HEAD

stories

William Tester

Winner of the 1999
Mary McCarthy Prize in Short Fiction
Selected by Amy Hempel

Sarabande Books

LOUISVILLE, KENTUCKY

LIBRARY OF CONGRESS CATALOGING-IN-PUBLICATION DATA

Tester, William.
    Head : stories / by William Tester.
        p. cm.
    "Winner of the 1999 Mary McCarthy Prize in Short Fiction
selected by Amy Hempel."
    Contents: Wet — Where the dark ended — Whisperers —
Bad day — Immaculate — Cousins — The living and the dead
dead — Floridita — Who's your daddy now? — Us.
    ISBN 1-889330-48-5
(alk. Paper)
    1. Young men—United States—Fiction. 2. Fear—Fiction.
3. Psychological fiction, American. I. Title.

PS3570.E85 H43 2000
813'.54—dc21   99-059918

Cover photograph: *Soap Pope*, by Josefa Mulaire. Provided courtesy
of the artist.

Jacket design by Josefa Mulaire.

I wish to thank the National Endowment for the Arts, the Constance Saltonstall Foundation, the Virginia Commission for the Arts, and Virginia Commonwealth University for their generous support. I would also like to thank Sarah Gorham and Amy Hempel, Kirby Gann, Nickole Brown, Charles Casey Martin, Tobias Wolff, Michael Martone, Melanie Rae Thon, Georges Borchardt, Gordon Lish, Peter Christopher, Roberta Bernstein, Diane Williams, Kathryn Staley, Paul and Phyllis Mulaire, Katherine and David Springstead, Charles and Delphia Womer, and Josefa Mulaire for their kind assistance with this book.

For Josefa and Dante

ACKNOWLEDGMENTS

I wish to thank the editors
in whose magazines these stories first appeared.
"Bad Day" was first published in *TriQuarterly*;
"Where the Dark Ended" in *Black Warrior Review*;
"Us" in *The North American Review*; "Wet" in *Witness*;
"Floridita" in *Fiction*; "Who's Your Daddy Now?"
as "Shade" in *Story Quarterly*; and "Cousins" in
Esquire. "Whisperers" will appear in the
online magazine *Nerve*.

CONTENTS

"There was a time when I was really, truly alive, while it seemed only dead people walked by on the sidewalk." That is the first line of one of the stories in this collection, and the moment I read it, I remembered the *first* time I had read it—nearly two years earlier, in the *Black Warrior Review*. That moment of recognition occurred again as I read "Wet," a story I'd never forgotten after first reading it in *Witness*. This meant that, though I was reading manuscripts without names, I knew who the author was, and that his novel, *Darling*, published by Knopf in 1992, was a singular, stunning work that I often recommend to students and friends. I expected a lot, then, from the rest of William Tester's collection.

Head is a loosely linked group of stories that tracks a former farm boy from the Cracker Florida swamps through the wilder days of his youth, and notably through his shy, blundering romances. His mentor might have been T. W. Adorno, who famously said, "Of the world as it exists, it is impossible to be enough afraid." People speak of stories and novels as being "plot-driven" or, say, "voice-driven." If anything, Tester's stories are *fear*-driven. "Am I ever as scared as then? Back then I was made out of insects, which threatened to anytime take off and fly" ("Where the Dark Ended"). There is, in these stories, fear of women—each jittery flirtation an agony of nervous desire—fear of a cruel stepfather who routinely endangers his stepsons, fear of one's prospects. There is fear of the very act of speech, given the narrator's ruinous stutter. Yet it is the resulting clumsiness—the missteps, the need so great—that seduces us in ways some smooth operator could not. As Barry Hannah said in an interview in *Mississippi Review*, "Dylan can't sing, but he had the desperation of not being able to sing which is better than, say, Glen Campbell, who can sing."

In *Head* (and in what's going on *in* this fellow's head), there is a hierarchy of fear, as when the fear of being struck by lightning in a swamp trumps two brothers' fear of their stepfather who is forcing them to lay "barbwire" during a storm ("Wet"). Tester is good at the close call; in "Bad Day," the narrator floats in the Atlantic off the Florida coast: "A fin caught me, scraping my ribs like a Frisbee.... Its undersea, uncolored shape rubbed by me the length of a Chevrolet, and brushing by, pushed me as if to say, *Swim it! This is life. Swim, you idiot, swim.*"

Tester's characters look closely at what is available to us all; additionally, they often look at things they are not meant to see. They can't quite keep themselves from watching people in apartments across the way—a young woman toweling herself after a bath, for example, or an elderly couple, naked, demonstrative: "They both weren't pretty anymore. But it *still* was sex."

From hard physical labor in the steamy heat of the Florida "Glades" to trying to pick up women in New York City, Tester manipulates *event* with the best of them. But what carries the day is what his characters *make* of what happens to them: "Human consciousness," Rick Moody writes in *BookForum*, "is literature's true birthright—the shape and arc of interior life—no matter what your MFA friends tell you." Tester makes the smallest gestures worthy of our attention; he says something about the human condition even in the serving of a cup of coffee in a diner, "the chrome-edged, waitering boredom of it."

But Tester's language, the *way* he says it, is what it's all about. Where a lesser writer might say, "I was very frightened," Tester says, "I was never not mostly afraid." How to explain the thrill of coming across a line like that! His narrator, a halting sensualist, remembers the first woman who "killed" him, how "one of her hairs lay across the white bed in its gene-loaded curl." Describing a provocative cousin whose "fitty laughter purls a sound up in her mouth" to New York City tourists "dressed in pastels like big babies," Tester consistently catalogs the world in ways we haven't heard before.

I telephoned Tester at his home in Virginia to put a single question to him: I wanted to know the impulse behind these stories, what kicked things off. His answer came in two parts. He cited Isak Dinesen's comment about starting a story from a tingling feeling a certain memory gave her, then Faulkner's image of a girl-child with dirty panties in a tree. "It's somewhere in between those," he said. Then he told me what Denis Johnson said when he asked him the same question: "Man, I just had these memories of things that I didn't want to forget, and I was forgetting them."

Some time after the close call with the shark off Daytona Beach, Tester's narrator recalls the moment so intensely that he seems to be there again. It is not unlike the last lines of a poem by William Stafford:

". . . What you fear
will not go away: it will take you into
yourself and bless you and keep you.
That's the world, and we all live there."

Tester says it more starkly: "I'm like anyone. I'm still
scared, but I lived." He is saying something true here,
and in every one of these remarkable stories.

—Amy Hempel
New York City
April, 1999

HEAD

Wet

Like it wants something, barbwire bites at my T-shirt
and nicks my belly and my chest. But I take an end, lug
up a roll with my brother. We heft the barbwire into our
truck. The bed shudders—our truck has its own mind
too, just like everything. Even my thin freckled arm.

I leave the barn, blink at the soggy green land on
our farm with the palm trees' breezing fronds. Junk is
everywhere. What doesn't still need to sleep? Already,
the sun seems to vaporize last night's rain into a visible
greenhouse heat, and everything glistens, or wavers, and
steams a little.

"You're pickled. Sit, Snow White," Jim says. He tells me, "Easy, Hercules. I got it."

"I'm not all that awake," I say, and sip at a bottle of warm Coke by the truck.

"I'm good," he says. "You rest your drawers a minute."

Jim means it. He's shirtless, tanned and knotted and has a copper circling of hair around dark nipples on his chest. Wet lines of sweat run down his stomach. It's cooler inside our tin barn, shaded, and I sit with my hangover across a hay bale and watch how Jim talks with the wire, familiarly, used to big tools and to working—but he will suddenly, like our dad would, haul off and beat at some machine. I remember this one old Polaroid picture: Jim has the smirking, dented eyebrows that our younger father had.

I'm still tipsy, and Jim just keeps loading the wire. On most weekends our stepdad, Lloyd, doesn't wake all that chipper himself. He'll rub his big belly and tell me, *Modern days, you got to be scheming and spending just to show you're still afloat.*

You can't bullshit a bullshitter, he says.

A smell of mouse steams up when I turn a roll. There are three nude, baby, pink mice. They're blind, asleep, and twitch like fingers, and I have to dry heave over a bale.

"Know what I think? You ought to eat some sandwich," Jim says, and he nods to a plate on a rusting barrel with his white bread and ketchuped eggs. I'm nicked as shit, but barbwire never scratches Jim. He cleans and jerks a roll out in a slant of barn-door sun. I see him practicing baskets at school. Always far from me. Greasering under his car hood. Bad in math, smirking—that's how he is.

And who's this squirt?

That's Nim, my brother. Jim takes me cruising, drinking beer.

We meet girls at night, girls who he says will swim naked.

I try to help. Things could be worse, I figure. The rain last night maybe broke the drought. Maybe not. The palm trees in back of our barn lean with a breeze, but our land is blasted. I could be dead, I guess, or stuck here sweating without a brother. I pull my gloves off, and it feels like I'm peeling away heat. "It's useless. I'm no good at this farm shit," I say. "I give."

"I got it. Why don't you rest your head," Jim says.

I say our dad wouldn't be working us raw like this.

I ask why are we working so hard when it looks like it's going to rain. Gray hills of cloud float over our fence line, piling up.

Jim says, "Either way. We get the dried end of the lake fenced off, and the rest of the weekend's fishing. Now Dad's city kids, what can they do down there in Miami? *We* can take the boat, hunt if we want or whichever."

In a swamp, I think.

All morning everything watches me. I'm hungover as hell. I sit still on a hay bale, dreading work, a heave rolling up in my stomach, then I see our stepdad's hatted shadow cross the ground past the door of the barn. I go grab wire.

The shadow talks.

"You boys having a problem?" Lloyd says.

We look at each other like we don't know what, but that's okay, because all the wire is loaded, all our tools. Our little sister packed our cooler with sodas.

Lloyd blocks our doorway scraping his boot heel. He is big as sin. "You're about green in the gills," he says, and thumps me in the ribs. Lloyd gingers off his Stetson, fans. Then uses it to silently count out rolls of the loaded wire. "All righty, that lake ain't getting no drier. If you girls are ready to work," he says.

Wet

I sit in the rushing truck wind by my window faking sleep, but even with my eyes closed I know all the curves and stop signs, every tremble of change in the roads. Smooth blacktop, whispering gravel, macadam. In the swimming red-blackness behind my eyelids I know *here's* a truck-stop parking lot and *there's* a grove of lemons. I lose my grip sometimes and sleep, but I don't like it—and I wake with a spot of my drool on Lloyd's arm.

Lloyd passes wind. "Listen to that alligator yawp," he says. His face is unshaven, and some whiskers glint clear with an inner light.

Lloyd likes to keep me up front in the cab with him, to split us up. Past the shotgun rack and the window, Jim rides crouching in the truck bed with Sherman and Abe to keep those red hounds in, so I lean farther out. I lean as if only looking and spit a thin, long stream of bile. Abe sniffs at it, interested. I see Jim yelling something at me, but his sound all dissolves in a wash of wind. With their noses up, our dogs wait for me to spit again.

I can taste something like silver, a smell of beer.

"God, when'd you all get to bed?" Lloyd says. He shakes his head and reaches for a packet of cheese crackers on the dash. "I catch you all out drinking, and me and your mama'll whip your ass. Say, tell the truth. You weren't out chasing those split-tails, were you?" He grins.

I see me sitting last night in Jim's Nova. We're at Ocala Lake. The tape deck is going, and while Jim is parked off in Regina's car, I'm drinking his six-pack of Coors. I'm bored, and I'm muggy, and my throat is tight. I pop a beer. Rain rumbles out on the wind-shield. A car door light blinks on outside, streaked with rain, and two girls run off to another car. I thought, what could I say to those girls? One was laughing, her clothes blue as milk in the darkness.

I could have driven on home on my learner's, but what was at home?

Green-fruited orange groves line the highway, and in the new housing development behind the groves, a water tower is painted to look like a golf ball on its tee. "God a' mighty, look! Look at that Yankee shit," Lloyd says.

My temples are roaring and I would rather not talk to him. I try to look grim and nod.

"So-called real estate. . . . Guess you two studs have been out all night drinking? Like I can't tell," he says. "Well, if you're pukey, there's some Old Crow under my seat, here." He spooks me by reaching over quickly to squeeze my knee. Lloyd yawns, rubbing his whiskers, then he glances over and sees I've flinched. He wins. Lloyd's not that bad, but I think despite himself, fear gives him some small sense of pleasure. It's a kind of awe.

His eyes go dead and shiny, and he waves a big tanned arm at the world. "Paving everything. Soon won't be nothing left," he says.

I nod, but we're off to fence his lake in.

We stop for gas at Stuckey's, and when I come back from getting sick in the men's I see three city children in matching clothes walk up to look in our truck. They're Miami types, fish-belly white, and they poke at things. Jim lets them, his back to the kids while he pumps the gas.

Then Jim says our dogs will bite their hands off.

No way, the kids tell Jim.

"Well?" he asks me.

"Every finger," I say. "Go ahead."

Our other land is swamp and jungle. There's no land, just trees and overgrowth of vines, and green palmettos, roots and cypress, muck and ferns and moss and mushroom clusters—there's no earth, but what there is is lush and pretty. We bump down a weedy trail through a moss-hung tunnel beneath the trees. The dead gray moss blocks almost everything, fluffing across our windshield like a solid mossy wall or like the ragged clothes of ghosts. Big white magnolia flowers hanging low enough to hit our truck hood burst apart when we drive by the branches, scattering leaves and long white blossoms that slap like hands against the glass. From inside it is a wonder, with spiders and speckled emerald lizards falling all over and our dogs straining and snapping at stuff in the back.

Out here, everything is sweaty or bites or is dying. In a steamy heat.

Lloyd pulls up through a clearing. Where we are is the wooded end of a bean-shaped lake. It is mostly marsh, and it is ready to be grazed to the water. Right now though, the cows haven't wrecked it, and it's peaceful here, totally wild. You could lie down and practically sleep, but Lloyd and Jim would see. "Sleepy, here, still needs his nap," they'd kid. I sit up.

Lloyd parks on the marsh bed down by our metal boat. We're stopped, but I still feel the wind, its static. The air has a charge, and the far end of the lake is now rimmed with those pearly gray mountains of cloud. Like the bomb was dropped.

Lloyd says "You boys don't start playing. We're here to work."

I think to myself, what a jerk. I look back at our two dogs wagging their bodies entirely, grinning back. The dogs are foolish and all jumped up. Lloyd gets out and steers Abe's nose to the waving sawgrass while he points at nothing much. *"Go get 'em,"* Lloyd whispers, and the dogs leap out there running. Our dogs are gone.

I follow Lloyd and Jim a hundred yards out where our fence ends, down to the brace posts sunk in the weedy marsh. Lloyd squishes out onto cattails. I act interested and drag out the crowbar we use to spool wire.

Jim says, "It's rained here, too," and he kicks the muck. "The water's high. This land's still as wet as my pecker."

Like Lloyd, Jim's guessing, since no one can see for the swords of grass. It could be millions of years ago here, all the dragonflies. Sawgrass is thick as dry wheat. Things flit and swarm at my forehead. "And it's buggy, man."

"So. Now we're here. . . . We're laying fence," says Lloyd. "This little swamp pond will dry up directly."

Lloyd takes his hat off as if it would help him to think. On a map this lake shows bigger, but Lloyd says when a drought settles in on North Florida the lake goes dry for years. Lloyd buys the shoreline strip of cheap forest, to the waterline. If the lake shrinks small, Lloyd tells us, then two hundred curving acres of shoreline will dry into a *thousand* acres of land. New, sawgrassed, grazing land for cattle. "We fence this end of the lake, and it's our'n. You follow me?

See, your smart man will think so he won't have to work, he says.

"We'll lay that barbwire, razor tight, right on the top of the water. Just a single strand . . . won't even need us no posts."

Jim says, "But the lake makes a fence, you ask me."

"Well, knothead, next time I'll *ask* you. How's that?"

I sneer at Jim. Lloyd yanks my T-shirt, and we follow him out where the lake is marsh. I nod like I'm listening, but I'm gone again.

—Last night, they were out in the rain, looking for beer. I called to them. One girl laughed out in the darkness, running car-to-car. "She let me, Nim. I screwed Regina," said Jim.

I could tell he did.

Out on the marshy grass, I watch a swamp rabbit slip through palmetto shoots. I think, if Lloyd wasn't here, I'd blast that swamp rabbit all to hell.

Lloyd brings me back to him. "She's drying fine. Look it here, look how much field we could claim. Now you all go load up your boat. Take that crowbar, and spool up your barbwire out from the *boat* back."

"The boat," I whisper. "Are you kidding?"

I aim the crowbar at Lloyd's back like he's a rabbit.

"Yeah, you all go bring up the boat," Jim says, but not where Lloyd can hear him.

I go with Jim. It's not that I care where we lay the fence. The thing is, my head's still banging, and I need to slow down our pace a bit. The air trembles. I tell myself I shouldn't drink. *I can't drink*, I say, and I think about sneaking a nip of Lloyd's liquor, a Sprite even. I whisper, "Why don't we just lay the fence where the lake is *dry*."

"That'd be too simple," says Jim.

"It sucks," I say, then I knock it off, hearing myself.

I help my brother upright our small rowboat. A heat pours out, sickening us. Where the boat laid up draining, the grass is bleached, making a shadow boat.

Yellow-green. Bugs flick up in the spiky grass, and from everywhere crickets and frogs and cicadas hum, droning. The sound wants to buzz from inside your head. Then it feels like wet sand in my mouth—like I'll lose my lunch, and I sneak to the pickup and fish under the seat for Lloyd's whiskey, but I chicken out.

"Well, tiger, you look good," Jim says. "The Living Dead. Why don't we just fucking shoot you." We drag the boat out from under the tree line and up to the marsh where the lake water starts. We load it up, aluminum buckling and popping. No one talks.

I think back to when we were small. Our dad would take my sister Jane and me and Jim fishing. Jane and I always got sick. Or I'd hit her. Once I was afraid to bait crickets, and I dropped their butter tub in the water where they got away. *"Fuck it. Forget it,"* Dad said, and he took us home, knuckling the plasticky steering wheel, choking it. Now Dad is different. He has other kids, and I think about living with him in Miami.

Dad could drive up and come save us.

But I know I'm dreaming. I will never go.

Lloyd sort of hops in the little boat and feeds out a loose end of barbwire.

I take it, and when the thunder hits, each of us leaps back a step from the wire and a thunder sound hums through our fence post and down the fence, rumbling us.

"—That liked to scared me, no shit!" says Jim. "I'd say it's fixing to storm."

Lloyd looks at his boots in the boat floor. They are rubber-soled, and he glances above at the weather. "Fine," he says, satisfied. "It'll cool us off good if it sprinkles. We leave now, and some *rich* man'll come put up a fence. Now you all come back here and push us off," and his mouth seems to stiffen like another Lloyd, serious.

Through cattail reeds and sawgrass, I see water where muck has been. I see where the rain has filled our old shoreline, in tea-colored ponds. But we tiptoe in. Jim and I push, and a smell steams from under the boat, something sulfury, duckweed and pond scum and rotting fish. My boots sink, and Lloyd dips his oars in the sawgrass and tries to row.

Aluminum warbles and scrapes the grass.

Across the marsh, sawgrass bends tan on the water and a breeze stirs up, cooling us. Lloyd slaps his oar at some cattails. "Keep pushing! This mother won't row yet," he says. "If it storms, we'll quit."

We shove him off, but the boat will not move through tall weeds.

Lloyd curses and slams the old oar down, and unrolls more wire to give us slack. It jumps as it kinks and uncoils. We push him about ten feet out in the water, then Lloyd seems to read us—to be *measuring* Jim, and his face takes a sheen of fine sweat.

"... Better yet," Lloyd says, "why don't you all stay out and just *push* the boat."

I don't get him. I stand around looking when I understand Lloyd. It's his other voice.

"Could yall wade?" he says. *"Marsh here is too thick to paddle. If the water gets high we'll row her, but not till we're pushed past this sawgrass.* You follow me? Well *come on,* girls. I don't mean starting tomorrow. Push!" he says. "I can't row this some-bitch, and sit here, and lay out the barbwire both."

So we wade the lake slogging through water, kind of waking me, and my knees disappear in brown silt.

Jim whispers, "We'll all be lightninged. We're gator bait."

"It sucks," I say. "Why doesn't it just start to rain?"

"—I tell you what. Why don't you all do what I

goddamn ask!" Lloyd answers. "And I'd keep my boots on for snakes. Now let's see how far you can wade the boat. Push, damn it."

Unkinking, the barbwire rolls out between us like a giant spring, and I suddenly slip in mud to my waist. "Whoa! Wait," I say.

Lloyd snatches the uncoiling wire aside. "Good Christ!" he says, hovering his big, hatted bulk at me. "All right you sissy, get in! *Get in . . . ,*" he yells. *"Get in the fucking boat."*

Thunder comes, murmuring again, moving like stereo over the water. It is all around.

"Believe this shit? Go ahead, Skinny, get in. Get in!" says Jim, holding the boat. "The lightning will kill us, if we don't sink."

Now I'm too scared not to listen to Lloyd, and I climb on into the boat.

My brother stays pushing; he wades the lake, moving us, sliding our boat across deeper glade. Before us the lake is a maze of marsh, walls of tall sawgrass. And rain coming.

Lloyd hands me an end of the crowbar, and we lay the wire.

"Push it, Jim! Look at your big brother work," Lloyd says to me. "Ain't you ashamed *even a bit?*"

I want to answer him, *yes.*

■

Behind all these gray clouds above us, the lake has a long purplish curtain like night coming, but it's just noon. We hit clear water, and Jim climbs in and starts rowing. He is sopping wet up to his chest. A mile away, heat lightning strikes on the farthest shore. Flickering white.

"Boy, hold that crowbar," Lloyd says, and he slaps my head.

An egret unfolds and flaps softly across the green water lilies, toward the shore, and into the moss of our forest. Then the air rumbles closer. It thunders, and for a second we stop like our dogs will, and get back to work. Cattails surround us, then pass.

—I'm fading. I almost puke holding the wire up. It coils out shining and quickly sinks.

Jim drags his oars at the weeds, and the oars wing up, dripping with green rags of lily pad, bogging up.

"Damn it to hell. We're all stuck again. Move," says Lloyd.

Jim rows harder, only rocking us. "I'm caught," he says, catching his breath.

"Idiot."

I think, *you gob of spit*, and imagine us shotgunning Lloyd on this swamp somewhere, then a big, purple, darkening curtain draws over, and a drop of ice plops on my shoulder, and some smaller drops, clapping the water like shattered glass, and all at once it starts to rain.

It roars on us.

Rain splotches over Lloyd's shoulders and molds his clothes.

"Jesus, God, give me a break," he says. "Idiots!"

Rain makes Jim's hair wet and flattens his head to a smaller head. A smaller him.

The rain pours down heavier, in a wall of wet. Rainwater runs on our faces and drums the boat. I'm dying. The wire is so heavy it feels like my fists have fused over the crowbar. They are throbbing white.

Lloyd says, "Yall are so lazy... it's not worth my effort to whup your ass." Lloyd's shirt is soaked. He shifts around trying to figure and nicks his fist, which pinkens with rain and thin blood.

"I can't *ever* get nothing to work!" he yells.

"Nothing, I swear it! I'm getting wet," and he hefts me the full weight of the wire.

It breaks me, *wham*, and the wire drops past me and dents the floor.

"*Sissy boys*, give me a try at those oars," Lloyd yells, and I watch my brother wince. Lloyd rises and crabs around standing, and shimmies the boat in the water, nearly tipping us. "Shit," he says, "I'm too big," and he sits on the boat wall and grins.

Then I'm scared again. I watch Jim chew at his cheek. I have seen this look. He just sits. In thunderclouds flickering with lightning, we sit in our boat on the lily pads, rocking a little, surrounded by tall walls of sawgrass and bearing the rain like our blinking dogs.

Not a mile away, lightning falls zigzagging, and I totally let go of the crowbar. Conductivity. I think of water and science. The rainwater pools where my wire roll dented the boat hull. Electric things. "See, Jim," I mutter to him. "He don't care."

"Hell's bells," Jim says, and he stands to pole. "Okay," he says, passing an oar to me. "Then pole it when *I do*," he says. Jim poles hard and the boat lifts, rocking us, and I take up the oar and start shoving, but we barely go. Jim heaves. We're moving, and it looks like to me that my brother is not so much poling the boat, as he is dragging the whole lake beside us, like a giant rug.

Then we stop.

"That's it," Jim yells. "Molasses. She's fucking stuck."

Lloyd bends to slacken the wire.

Jim says, "Couldn't we *just back up* and row in?"

Lloyd squints his face toward the rods of rain. His Stetson drips thin streams of water. Above us the storm howls and rains in tons, flooding our boat.

"We could try, but we'd lose all that wire," Lloyd says. "It'd get all bunched up," and around him the sound is of thunder, and a roaring splash.

"I can't," Lloyd says, finally. "Not at fifty-five dollar a roll."

We squat there not moving, and then I sit.

"... No way in hell," he says.

The rain drifts in big sheets and veils of wet, raising a staticky roar of white noise. I start to like the sound, and behind the clouds, I can see lightning. It is beautiful, following us, like we are being eaten alive.

I realize my head is fine. I don't feel a headache.

"He'll have us fried," Jim says, huddled.

Lloyd plays his hand at the water like a swimming fish, and the forest clouds flicker with lightning. He grins at Jim. *"Look, son, it's really not all of that deep,"* he says, working on us, greasy, and he tips the wet front of his hat brim to dump the rain. Lloyd starts with Jim, hunkering down.

Lloyd says, "The lightning's quit over us. Say, Jim, why don't you get in the water and *push* again? Why don't the *two* of you get in and *push us.*"

"Yeah, if *you* cut the wire," Jim says.

Lloyd bows his head. "All right," he says, nodding a bit.

Maybe there isn't anything in that world. But the shadowed lake looks at us, pocked with rain, and the three of us look back into its darkness.

I touch the lake and notice it's warmer, then my hand jerks back from the lily pads feeling that something moved under the water, that it senses us, and Lloyd and Jim can see I got scared. I hear myself think *don't give in.* Don't show them you know that you've flinched.

I dip my hand back in.

I tell myself something our dad had said, *Touch the bait, son.* We were fishing then, *touch the bait, son . . . it won't kill you. Anyhow, you won't be scared if you're dead*, or it could have been something else like this. Or a different day. But that was him, while I know that something in the lake, here, will *kill* me.

Electricity. I touch my hand at the water.

I'd rather let it, I think, than to be scared of Lloyd.

I put my oar down. I squish off my boots and jump in.

"Yeah, buddy, swim!" says Lloyd. "Push it boy."

"Hell if *I'm* stupid," Jim yells. "It's too stormy, man." But after Jim says this he drops his oar, takes off his boots, and slides in.

"Just shut the fuck up," he says, swimming. "You think I'd just sit there with him?"

Where my face breaks the water, the lake is the color of iron and the rain is gray.

Lightning hits. A slash of white over our shoreline. I feel thunder thump under the water, and around my feet, it quivers the rubbery-stalked lily pads.

"Ignore it, boys," Lloyd yells. "See them tall cypresses? We're not the highest thing here. Push," he says.

Down in the lake water, the sound of the rainfall surrounds me and pats my head. My chin parts the duckweed and hyacinths, lily pads, their flooded leaves sunken, or floating just under the lake in a film of rain. Jim and I swim back and paddle.

I count the light flashes and wait for hot lightning to glow down our fence somewhere, boiling us. I won't give up, I think, *swim*.

Lloyd rolls the wire and we push the boat, kicking again at the lake bottom, and I slog through what feels like a soup of snakes, cottonmouths. Leaves that fold over and mold my arms.

Lloyd still leans over us, fencing. His hands are nicked, shaking, and he jerks a hand back when the lightning hits.

A fizz fills my ears for a second. But I've gotten used to the lightning. I expect the flash, and I can hear rain patter under the water. Holding me, mud sucks and floods as I kick it, and loads my clothes. We swim twenty-odd feet through wet greenery, and I see what at first is a floating log, then I see it's the brown, swollen back of a gator and panic runs over my stomach and down my legs, jolting me, and I see that it's just an old car, just a rusty old car sunk out in the water, mostly rounded roof. Its windows are gone, but the hood is up, yawning high, lipping out over green lake moss. I see bullet holes. Torn places punched through the rust.

We swim the boat forward and paddle close. It's a ghost bucket. Where the car windshield should have been, a turtle head floats on the water. I imagine the car is all full of them, thousands there, their leggy shells saucering around underwater and between my knees.

Instantly the turtle head sucks back under the lake. The car creeps me out, and I shiver still. Jim stops swimming and holds the boat, watching the old car in the water.

"Keep pushing, hey!" While Lloyd pokes an oar at the rusted hood, crumbling it, I peek up. I chin myself over the boat hull and see some trees. I see the south fence and the other end. Our forest, our fence, and the shoreline.

"Jesus," Lloyd yells, "look at that! I'd make it to be like a Edsel. Say a 'fifty-eight."

I feel something staring, aware of me. We swim by the ghosts in the Edsel, and its shaded old car windows watch as we pass.

"—Jim," I say into the rain. "We'll get killed like this."

"I know," he says. "Barbecued."

Lloyd tips for a second and rights himself, shouting at us, "Push, damn it."

The raindrops fall swollen and form plate shapes that rattle the water.

I stop shaking, and a current like lead fills the air. The sky turns a gray like the lack of good color, and the rain doesn't let up, but the weak are forgiven, and I know the absolute bomb is falling, or something like that, really big.

The tallest dead cypress tree shakes on our shoreline. It glistens. From the highest fork, a branch snaps and drops from this cypress and the air flickers glowing and lightning slams, shaking the boat, and the rain gets a smell like there's roasting sap.

"Forget it!" Jim says. "I mean, Jesus . . . I thought you were cutting the wire, Lloyd."

"Don't pussy out on me. Push!" he says.

Jim whispers, "Why aren't *you here*, pushing us."

My fillings taste bitter.

I count off in thousands and wait for it. I count the calm, a space in the air like remembering, and in my face, a white arc of light flares the water. Lightning hits. A column so white it is almost blue. In front of me, smoke circles up from a stand of palms, and the sky flickers, quickening, and the air on my face feels like satin.

The next time it hits it is quiet, then the day goes impossibly white.

The air explodes, slamming like gunshot.

Jim stops to see if Lloyd is serious.

I watch the men.

"Lloyd," Jim says, whispery. "Okay now, Lloyd, it is lightning us."

Lloyd rolls the end of the wire out. He ties the free end to our final roll, and spools up one last roll of the wire.

He lays it out.

"Then you better push *faster*," he says.

In the rain last night, Jim woke me up when the girls went home. The windows were fogging, and I forgot I was there in his Nova. "Hey," he said, the rain hung in beads from his open door. "Who drunk up all of my Coors?"

I woke up then, wanting a beer. "Not me," I said. I was scared.

"Looks like you've had you a party. . . . Who you been doing, Slick? Anyone?"

I told my brother zilch.

"Get real," he said. "What are you waiting for, Christmas?"

It was me and Jim. I remember they laughed on the water. I'd heard them swimming in the lake somewhere. When the girls ran by, I called, *Hey, listen*, but no one turned. I knew no one could hear through my car door, the rain falling. I pretended I didn't care. There were other girls. One was naked. They were white as ghosts out in the rain.

Out in the moss and weeds, I let the boat go and swim.

"Jim," I say, swimming away, "I'm going in. I'm too spooked for this."

"No shit?" he says. "Serious."

"Really, Jim. If I leave," I say, "what are you thinking you'll do?"

"He'll beat your ass."

"It won't be as bad as the lightning."

"God, screw it," Jim says. "He can't kill us."

"He wished he could."

"—What are yall saying?" Lloyd says.

I swim away from there. I don't care. "Hit me," I tell him. "I'm going in."

I hear Jim splashing and look back at him. He

shoves the boat roughly, and swims to my side of the wire. Then Jim blows his nose as he surfaces. "Lloyd, I better help him. It's too deep," he yells, and Jim swims away from the boat.

"I dare you! I *dare* you to try it, you little shit."

I hear my brother, Jim, swimming behind me.

"I'm going home to call Dad. I'm too scared," I say, and that's how we leave the man sitting, the boat gleaming wet in the water. Electrified.

When we reach the trees' canopy, passing as if through a smaller storm into the rain broken under our forest, it's another world. The trees are green and everywhere dripping. Their leaves shelter us, while the rain and the lake are like night outside, a grassy field troubled with lightning. We walk sodden under dripping magnolias, huge cypresses, and onto a trail at the forest edge. A dog is there. Abe crouches crying and shivering, holding his tail hooked between his legs. Coming in, we find Sherman hiding under our pickup. Jim asks, shouldn't we swim back and help him, and he peers for Lloyd out by the sunken car. "He'll kill us," Jim says. "If the lightning quits."

"Yeah, but what if it doesn't," I say.

Across the lake, clouds make a cave on the tilting

grass, marsh grasses, darkening now with black water, where it's flooding back.

Jim climbs up on the truck hood. When he spots the boat, the first thing Jim says is Lloyd's hat is gone. When I see him, his head is bare, glowing and rained on, and his shirt is off, but Lloyd is still poling the boat. Like he'll never quit. I count off in thousands and listen. I count the calm. Behind us a wind sweeps the forest, and I'm wide awake. A shatter sound passes the tree leaves, the rain falling, thunder, and pattering water. I find the Old Crow and we crack it. We watch Lloyd forcing the boat. I let our dogs shove into the truck with us, and I wait for what all will hit next.

Where the
Dark Ended

There was a time when I was really, truly alive, while it seemed only dead people walked by on the sidewalk. It snowed that night, fluttering outside like big fallout, and I followed these two stoned girls into the diner. I say girls since they, we, Leon and I, were not much more than twenty, twenty-four, and had just decided to hitchhike that night down to Cozumel, Mexico, or to anywhere. This was in New York. We were poor, and we didn't know where else to go.

What do I remember? Touching her. I took a booth, catching my thin face in the window as Britta and her blonde friend sat checking us out. They sat chain-smoking. If I could just touch her, I thought, I'd be saved.

I stutter some.

"Why do you stutter?" she said.

I was so nervous. I was never not mostly afraid. I didn't know we were all the same.

"I don't. Barely ever," I said. This was almost true. I only stuttered around grownups and women. Though for several years I had tried being an actor, which was stupid since I was unable to speak clearly at all in a crowd. Usually, I had to get drunk to be able to talk to a girl. Now I just stared, I guess. Her eyebrows were dark with a mink-looking thickness, and the truth is, all I could think of was sex. What else is it? We all know what hair really is.

My Southern friend, Leon, kind of stretched in his cheap leather jacket, and he and the blonde friend openly flirted. "Girl, you're too much," he said, things like that.

But I grinned at her stupidly, seeing Britta was braless through the weave of her sweater. Her skin was tan. So I acted cocky, and grinning to cover my shyness, I reached out and gently peeled open her hand.

"L-let's see," I said, touching her palm. "That's your

heart line. You know, I maybe knew you once, b-back in the past."

"Oh, you did," she said.

". . . I was taller, though."

The blonde friend, Debbie, asked, "Who was tall when?"

I squeezed Britta's hand. I felt my jaw shaking then.

"Now let's get this straight," Britta said. "Leon's the model, and which one of you has this old family place in the Keys?"

"Well, the Glades," I said.

"Glades," she said. She was one of those thick-haired young women you'd see around NYU, beautiful, while I was skidding around, poor as dirt, and trying to avoid having a job. Earlier, at the Mudd Club, I had asked her to dance and she danced with me. The thing is, she'd been watching me—and she knew I would—that's why I asked. I had shouted it over the music, in the strobing dark. Then the four of us left and walked down to this diner. It was New Year's day, 1979.

Disco was over and some newer dark time edged the city.

In our booth, Britta held Debbie's neck while she whispered some secrecy, and when I tried to listen to this whisper Britta saw through me. There was maybe this small wet thing that her lips did, their fattened bow, a tiny yet sensual motion, and I was undone. She just noticed me, and this shot-glass funnel of vision, surrounding us, peripherally blurred out the world.

Britta turned her hand over and closed her palm.

"My heart line," she asked me. "What else are you seeing, exactly?"

"Way, way, way not enough."

To touch her. The hot-water flood of her hands. The light of love. Any second, I knew she would get up and run.

"Hey," Leon said, "what the hell. Why don't we hitch out tonight? I mean not even pack."

"Oh, right," Britta said, "the four of us hitchhike tonight to Oaxaca."

"We could sit here and rot in this diner," I said, slipping far away.

Leon said, "I got a friend who could lend us his dad's old delivery van."

"You see?" I said.

"So what do *we* do?" Britta said. "Give you guys blow jobs, I guess, while you're driving?" Then her nails scratched my arm, leaving whitish scales.

I knew it then. But for all she knew we could have been killers. I could have been a monster who would work every horror on her, at my boiler pipes, naked in chains.

A few darkly dressed hipsters streamed into the diner, some old Ukrainian men, everyone still looking hungover.

As if tortured, our waiter walked over with coffee, his inner life, each and every wrinkle nearly screaming from the strain. You could tell that for years he had died at this job. Its sickening light, each evil plate and grinning sandwich. The chrome-edged, waitering boredom of it. Over and over it cut, this work, his death by little gestures in a nightmared karmic hell.

In a way, he was also myself.

"Here, kitty," said the pretty friend, Debbie, and dug in her purse. She unfurled a small pink palm full of LSD, in blotter tabs, stamped tiny faces on paper, Mighty Mouse, dozens of bright smiling cartoons. Her palm made a long-petaled flower.

"Whoa!" Leon said, and tore off a tab. "I know these guys. These little guys are old friends of mine." Then he took off his skull ring to try it on Debbie.

"Too loose," she said.

"—Not that *that* matters," Britta said. "Not to her, at least."

Under our rickety table, a socked foot touched my knee, and it rode my thigh, kneading me, then settled itself warm like a cat on the crotch of my jeans.

I swear, I thought maybe I'd come. My eardrums were roaring, but I just pretended to stir my hot coffee. I stirred all those small, floating, oily beads. Her foot kneading me. The thick red embarrassment plowing my body.

"Actually," Leon said, "hitchhiking might even be better."

". . . And l-less gas," I said.

Sure, they dumped us. Within minutes they went to the girls' room and ditched us. Richer friends came in. Guys in black coats, and tall women.

"We got to split. Hey, have fun in Oaxaca," they said, those killer queens.

"Wait," Leon said. "We'll come, too."

"No, we got to meet someone," Debbie said.

No, really, they said, and left us to run on the bill.

Of course, I could say this all totally crushed me.

But wasn't it also a kind of relief?

Later, when Leon and I were a lot drunker, we

would see them both beautifully seated at the One-Fifth Bar. Our Mexico girls were warm and pampered, stoned, while we slushed ice-pick cold through the street snow, smoking the windows, looking in. We were so timid. We didn't know to go in.

There were dozens, but this is the first woman who killed me.

Amazing, the intensity of living back then. Each night. First we drank, then we sat and had coffee. Around us, defeated old people like candle nubs, nothing-eyed, prayed to their cups in the diner. Formica, the table-ware and napkin bins, each grimly stainless surface breathing that hospital taste to the air. She went in me, way up inside of my mind, right there, our faces all lit up with wanting, clearly radiating light.

I knew it then.

"Why do you stutter?" she'd said.

This is the inevitable horror; this is your punishment for having lived: you want to, but you rarely remember her body, her shoulders. The walnut-shell-pallored

Sahara of her. A sand color. A fine blondeness swept down her small belly.

The breeze made these human ghost-shapes in her curtains when I saw them one morning, alone in her room. Her smell was there. One of her hairs lay across the white bed in its gene-loaded curl.

After they left, there was nothing much else but to live. So we both ate up our halves of the LSD, Leon and I dabbing our tongues with the tabs. I was stuck with him, outside, with the costumed, anesthetized drug-life of Washington Square, which was sadly trashed, beer bottles, confetti, dirty party favors, the New Year's mess. We sat back on the wall while I waited to get sick from it. I always did.

"Hell, I'm faking," said Leon. "I'm too tired now. You go on ahead," and Leon held out where his thumb hid his torn half-a-tab.

He hadn't even nibbled his acid. "No...you asshole."

"Oh, don't be so wimpy. You'll live. It's almost not even still dark," he said.

You could smell it, an exhaust-flavored whiff of the coming dawn. And with each breath of it I was more poisoned. Each step I was farther away from the girl. How hopeless! Then my vomit flew out. I was gagging. "I ought to go home and hide," I said.

"No, go with it. Totally, man."

I retched again. "I'm going to hide and not ever come out."

"Hey, don't waste it, Nim. Here, take my tab," he said.

"T-take yours," I said. "God, how is it I always get mixed in this shit?"

He yelled after me, "Oh, yeah. Everything's all fucked up cause of me . . . right? Every time."

I had to run somewhere to die. To shadows, if not to Cozumel, then to the waterfront. Anywhere. I had to walk off my high.

By the time I'd slushed to the end of the Hudson, the sky had become totally dawn in New York. Night, *God of all*, once more had drawn up his darkening wings. I listened, and pigeons, a dog, and a man in rags all seemed to mutter to each other some warning.

Burnt-up sun. That acid had maybe not taken its total effect as this was like any cold morning. Nothing sang. I slogged through the snow to New York's oily harbor, and my walk seemed like days. Yet it had only been minutes my watch tried to lie, conspiring. Yes, time in its ticking infinity unfolded, accordion-like in my mind.

—I thought, what if I saw her alone somewhere, and I could just kiss her and not have to *talk*? This is what stutterers all wished. It's what locked me up, the certainty that if I opened my mouth I would flub it. But she was far from me, by almost a day.

Before me, the Wite-out of snow smothered Battery Park with its shivering, leafless trees. These trees seemed alive to me, at the end of the end of the island. Behind me, the Trade Towers looked sun-bronzed and wavering. They were falling down, and each bit of light broke into rays. Electrically. Everything showed me its mind. This town was so old. It was tired, and weighed down as she was with her hideousness, I felt that New York only wanted to rest.

Some tourists came, dressed in pastels like big babies. There were foreigners, a drab seagull that eyed me with pity, poor creature. I knew everyone knew I was high.

Stalking eight o'clock, I bought a bottle of beer. It was meaningless, only six ever made any sense to me. As

I wandered, the seawater dipped and changed colors and swelled with a radiant and inner life. I began to premeditate every inhaling. I shocked myself, mirroring back from a car, all muscular. I felt glorious! New, with one beer. I would call the girl. But this was simply an adrenaline rush of false power. I would never call.

Then this bus load of screaming schoolchildren drove up with a tour bus of young Japanese. They surrounded me, touristing up from my dreams. They were one somehow. They knew why we were all here.

I tossed back my beer dregs and fondled the bottle. I was missing things—everyone watched the Atlantic:

An androgynous sea monster rose on the water, insanely sized, actually striding the waves.

Miss Liberty!

That big monument, it looked like her arm held the heart of a whale. Worn turquoise, she strode on our icy dark harbor, Miss Liberty, and whispered to me my need. Here the secret was, our great, draperied, crumbling colossus.

I had to go up inside her. It was clear to me. I had to climb up inside that idea. So I walked to the ferryboat, crushed up the gangway, and paid like the small Japanese. I could feel their telepathy. What a mutt I was. Surely they were superior. They were the future, with their common hair. I tossed my beer in the sea.

It felt cool, like the woods, in her body. A smell of paint. We all climbed the stairs up inside her, and in her crown, looked down upon the small world. We were all up there looking at death, I guess —swooning. Why, you could just climb out of this window and jump, I thought.

But what was Liberty like? I can hardly remember. When I looked at her she was alive with me, then when my thoughts wandered off some, she died. She swayed as the clouds hovered still in their heavens, all rusted and copper, our dead God.

Once ashore and sane, I stole a Heineken and walked on toward Wall Street, needing to smoke.

"H-hey, excuse me. C-could I borrow one of your smokes," I'd ask, clearly out of the fold, and confirming it.

The crowds surfaced. Now everywhere willed out of nothingness, there were the eager and hardworking dead again. Like Liberty, they knew the terrible secret here—you had to act, and I needed to finally do some-thing real.

So later I called her. I sat in my small tenement, the walls all around me on fire as I squeezed my amphetamined mind through the phone. Am I ever as scared as then? Back then I was made out of insects, which threatened to anytime take off and fly. She was smoking on the steps to her Hudson apartment. When she saw me I flinched. Britta had on this tie-dyed green T-shirt and sweater, her eyebrows blacked.

"You look like you're starving," she said.

I claimed that in fact I'd had several fine meals.

She drew in her cheeks with this Natalic Wood, actressy smirk. "You're all right," Britta said, "for a nervous wreck."

"Th-that's because you haven't seen me yet totally loaded."

We strolled from her stoop with my last twenty bills through the quivery world, that wild New York.

At the movies, her features flickered gray in the ghost light. I wanted to kiss her, yet I couldn't budge. What was that movie? It could have been God playing; I wouldn't have known, my eyes on her straight through the movie.

I was frozen up.

She turned to me, staring at her through the movie.

"What is it? *Just whisper,*" she said, and I stared at the glare on her neck. I could see her chest.

Before we walked back to Britta's apartment, we stopped to drink some fifty-cent beers at the Marlin Bar. You know the kind of place—the dust of a thousand loud years on its shamrocked walls, on bottle tops, and always that poor drunken kid with the sorrowful birthmark all over his head. Why was that birthmarked skin even there? What was it made of?

We leaned at the bar with a college crowd, drinking beer.

"Hey, back to Earth, why aren't you talking?" she said.

"What?"

"It's way too loud."

I almost reached out for her hand. I almost ran.

We glowed red in there, mirrored and lit with fluorescent gels.

"Then let's go somewhere quiet," I said. But I was too scared yet to kiss her, without several beers.

"Here, catch hold of my shirt while I get off this sweater."

I held her shirt, and the back of my hands touched her belly. Incredible, how warm it was. She gave me that grin again, burning. I wet my lips.

"W-wait," I said.

I leaned till my shoulder touched hers.

The crowd shifted. Dimitri, the blue-haired and giant old bartender, was wrestling a beer from the birthmarked kid's hand. He had grabbed an arm while the kid tried to suck down a Bud. "YOU. I'LL CUT YOUR HEAD OFF!" the man said.

"Wait, first let me get just a sip."

If I touched her, I reasoned, we could stand around, being there, quiet. Her beer glass sat beaded with these starry wet miniature bars. It was listening to us.

She leaned herself back on my arm. She saw me turn, then her mouth coming close, a small world. We kissed. Our futures exploding around us. I wanted to go up inside of her mouth totally and become her very tongue. Us circular, the way a vacuum cleaner inhales itself in the logic of cartoons.

"Whoa, hey," she said. Our teeth clicked together like seashelly things with the saltwater taste in our mouths. But did she see that I'd kiss her before I did?

I told her, "You, you already knew I was going to. . . ."

61

She touched my chin. I asked her why were we there, and we kissed some more. We moved our small romance to the dance floor. We hugged with our ribs in it. She and I kissed.

I knew it then.

She said, "Come and stay with me."

Britta kissed me again as we left, and she moved her wet tongue through my smile in the fine winter air. Gusts of snow fell across us. Darkness breezing over my bones. Tiny, ice-white stars shot above the apartments, and the same winking airplane that always is there.

What else can I tell you about how it went?

We walked on downtown to her river apartment. I got scared again.

"N-nothing's the matter," I said.

I tried kissing her. If only women knew how we were. How afraid we were. We leaned back against a parked taxicab, making out, and Britta put her hand in my pants.

"God, I'm sh-shivering."

"Yeah, but I couldn't tell," she said, "really."

I cupped her breast.

She tugged me, kissing.

"I'm so wet. Kiss me," she said.

We kissed in the light of her foyer and walked on inside.

I lit one of her cigarettes. "Do you have, like, anything at all here to drink?" I sat on her sofa and she brought in some beers.

"Be back in a second. I'm bleeding," she said, rising back from me.

"Where?" I said.

"What do you mean?"

I drew off her sweater and T-shirt. Her skin in light, blonde down the mound of her belly, the darker hair furring up under her arms. Britta kissed my pants.

"Don't move a muscle," she said, and walked off to a dark room down her hallway.

What sort of *things* were now down there? What waited for me down that hall?

Then I got undressed and in her bed, in the leaf-covered animal hovel I made of her covers on my skin. I don't know why she had thrown me. She wasn't perfect. She just did. While I waited. The musk of her sex staying damp on my hand, her woman smell. I could feel myself shivering.

Britta burned through the leaning soft light from

her bathroom, all naked, then in the darkness to me in her bed. She lay with the wool of her place by my body.

What was the dark like? Everything in the dark was . . . I don't know—more like what it truly is. Her torso and her arms were invisible. We hardly could see, in this blackness, that the other was more than just spiritually there, dim essences. We kissed again. In such darkness my limbs felt incredibly long. I couldn't tell where I was—or where the dark ended, and where I began. I touched at her skin. She held me, pinching. She licked at her hand and made both of us more wet, then my neck tensed up. She was too beautiful, even dark.

"What is it?" she asked me.

She kissed me, yet I couldn't think of our kissing. I wasn't there, all kinds of noise in my head. I could feel my heart. I moved on top of her, sweating—and cupped wetly half into her body, I slid inside, bending myself up in her, but terrored, and I collapsed limp in pure fear, my mind blazing.

". . . What's happened, what is it?" Britta whispered. "You've left."

I didn't say anything.

I didn't kill her and run.

"Nuh-nothing," I said. "It's the beer."

Britta eased from me. Both of us were naked as wood, that stillness. I didn't know what it was. So I lied to her. I was too scared to tell Britta. I wanted to fuck her, yet I couldn't budge.

We were lying there scared in her bed. I wasn't certain I would ever make love again, and that, I thought, would have been it, except that she kissed me. Britta pecked my chest. In the shadowing dark Britta's body rose, lifting a solid black mountain of sheet. A tent of her. I didn't know what it was she was doing. So I lay there and looked down at us astonished as she kissed my hips and belly. It felt as if someone had let go of my throat! Her hair in its cooling electrical movement, sparked with static. Pools of air. Her hair, our skin, and her breath on our bodies. She took me. Britta kissed me, my legs and my belly, and drew me in.

I suppose this is where I'm expected to put *I lived happily after that night*.

No, it's never fair.

But how must it feel to the dead?

What must it feel like to rise on the other side of life?

HEAD

In their long unaccounted grass avenues, the cemetery hills out in Queens stretch on for miles. Immense, vacant, gaudy high-rise apartments rise over Riverside Park, on up, past one-hundred-and-tenth to Harlem. The starved are in armies, and the Marlin, that bar is forever closed, crushed under concrete. These are things that never occurred to me in the daylight, and now I am older. My voice has cleared. Now those days are dead.

But we were young. We were very different than you or I.

The day came again and I left her place. My shoes went *crunch, crunch,* wet in the snow up on Broadway, away from her street and that time. Little did we know that nothing back then could be done again. It was behind us, that fun New York. That wilderness, smothered up white in a blizzard. God shook his big paper bag full of fallout. He intended to bury the wicked alive.

Before I left, I had lain there wanting to ask her. I could feel her breath.

She was half asleep. "Yeah, you can call me," she'd said.

But I never called.

Her dark hair fanned across the cold pillow. I saw her, and Jesus, God, her eyes.

I remember that, too.

I've said it, and I don't see what use there is in telling this again.

Whisperers

Summer came. We were down at our neighbors' place out by the lake, on a skinny dock. Half of the dock held their old bathhouse, and under us lake water lapped in the dark. The girls showered while I hid in the roof of the bathhouse. All our parents were gone, out at some juke for the night.

I climbed quietly, and chinned myself up in the rafters where no one could see. Not my little blonde sister, or our neighbor girls, Tanya and Kim—whose coppery brown hair showered flat down their backs. The taller one, Tanya, was fifteen or so, just like me.

HEAD

A tin-shaded light hung below me, and the girls held their towels or stood naked and splashed the floor. I had climbed up to change the burnt lightbulb; otherwise, the girls might have gone back inside the house. That whole evening we'd swam till the lake flecked with yellow-mooned water. Now the moon was gone.

No one saw. I mean, no one could guess I was still in the rafters. Then the girl I liked, Tanya, stripped off her wet one-piece. She was tallish and dark and her eyes were long, her mouth in a constant half-grin.

They talked, laughing and sharing the shower, their wet shoulders curved, muscular. Hidden like this, I was the monster we all feared in the darkness. I felt hideous, touched with disease. I felt wonderful!

Down in the bathhouse, my thirteen-year-old sister undid her bikini, and I almost fell. I jerked my head back as if I'd been slapped. My elbow knocked into the rafters—they heard me stir—and a whirl of dust tasting like cedar floated by me and was caught in the funneling light, dully glittering. Jane already had breasts and a crest of dark hair, like a little beard. I drew myself small toward the ceiling, behind the light.

They froze listening. My sister, Jane, turned off the shower, and no one spoke.

The shower thinned, dripping, and lake water echoed below us, some frogs throbbing. I heard my neighbor Ray's motorboat bump at the pilings, the shower drip.

Tanya looked up to the rafters and caught her breath. She was listening . . . looking right at me, but I don't know what all she saw.

They were tan and white.

I hid in the darkness and watched her. I made myself dark.

When I touched her, the lights were off all through their house. I could smell the lake. In my neighbors' dark living room, some of the dark things were like window shapes. Other shapes held themselves blacker—and apart from the windows and things of a lighter dark. I knocked into things, feeling about, lost in the house.

Shadow lamp. Rocking chair, stool, and recliner. A curtained wall. I inched around as quiet as snow.

Then I bumped the couch. "Hey, it's me," I said, and glimpsed the thin fog of her skin. I touched Tanya's hair and thin shoulders. She lay on the couch, bedded, and a sheet rustled.

I could make her out dimly. "You asleep?" I said, whispering.

Her father coughed somewhere, in sleep, and we went totally still.

"Come here," she said. "What do you think?"

We had been flirting all day at the lake . . . in the bathhouse shade . . . on the pine road out to the store . . . on the screened-in porch, mildewy. Wherever we could hide from our parents. I had fallen for her. I wanted to tell her some things. "I'll come see you tonight, if you want," I'd said.

"Okay, maybe," she had said. "Or maybe not."

Now I could hear Tanya sit up. We were shadow shapes, darker than ghosts. The air shifted, and Tanya was smiling, I thought, in the darkness. She took my wrist.

"Hey," she said.

"Did I wake you up?"

"Oh, not too much. Sit," she said, leading me, her voice going thin in a whisper.

I sat on the couch, creaking it. "I can't see you enough."

"Sh," she said. "Whisper."

She was leaning, I think, trying to see. Her hair had the smell of green water and the heat of the sun. She inched in and I slid next to her, touching.

"Why aren't you sleeping with them, with Jane and Kim?"

"*Sh*," she went.

"Listen, guess what," I said, "something I wanted to tell—"

"*Sh*," she said. "Whisper it into my ear."

So I whispered to her.

Then we kissed, and one by one, things seemed to shape themselves out from the darkness. The clouds passing . . . showing the fogged bulb of the moon. I could sense her eyes, window lit. The house turned from darkness to air, like the walls were back. Frogs and things amplified off in the night.

I was all lit up!

We touched in small motions like animals hunting.

"I can't see you," I whispered, and we kissed again. Everything dimly becoming blue silhouette, yet glowing somehow like a shadow. Above our couch, the stars and mooned night filled the window, now as bright as the lake.

I slid my hand down her satiny, warm panties. We were everywhere, night colored, her fingertips touching my stomach. She kissed my neck.

"*Sh*," she said.

I could barely see. But after a few tries we got used to it, moon on us. We were all lit up in the dark.

Bad Day

Sure, hysterically, I guess, I hid out again in the office stockroom so no one would see how I was. How messed up I was. Office air wore me out, every staple, every badly lit, Xerox-fumed breath I took. Since she'd dumped me, I could no longer look at my girlfriend, or anyone, without wincing straight in her face, whenever I passed one of them, the other beautiful record company people, in our tortured fluorescent-lit halls. I browsed and shook in my windowed stockroom, a lost closet crapped over with old, dead cassette tapes and compact discs overlooking forty-four leaning blue

stories of sickening, barely uninhabited air. Death
herself seemed to breathe right before me on the other
side of the glass—out beyond her, Central Park with
its carpet of trees, nearly night way up in Harlem. I put
my hand coolly against the window, feeling the wind
buffeting, trying to break in and get me.

Things were speeding up.

Who could say what all was wrong? It wasn't like
I'd had some big crisis, or anything—but for several
weeks I'd slept just miserably, sweating, and woke all
raw. Later, that morning, on my way to work, I kept
thinking the straphangers on the subway were too
aware of me, panhandlers, businessmen, all of them. I
should say screw it, I thought, and go home. Maybe call
in sick. But I fumbled around in my pockets, in my coat
even, and I couldn't find my damn keys.

I was *so* tired . . . for no reason it was starting to feel
like one of those mornings that are so impossibly over-
whelming, so nerve-racked, you just want to pick up
a gun.

I could do something like that, I imagined, if I got
thrown one more thing.

Around noon or so, I left the stockroom and went
back to work. Then I watched as Maria, my moody,

fellow tele-representative, walked my way down the Xerox hall, rubbing her dark eyes with a tissue wad. We'd had our moments, but we had never crossed over into romance, and so seeing her always stung. I copied things, poisoning my skin with the inky fumes. Words crossed her lips as she saw me, and I sensed a surge of telepathized anger vibrating between us down that hall.

"You're a tease," she would say to me. But if a woman came onto you, I felt some old order of things forced you to make a pass back. Once, I even believed she might go so far as to practice acts of magic or evil spells upon me, she being, they said, a witch. Maria and I'd had this half-hearted, sick flirtation, gazing at each other in meetings, or side by side, our arms brushing together in lust. Like me, I suppose she just needed to touch someone.

Now, as she came nearer, one of my eyelids began jittering wildly—I could hear my pulse, and my lips felt the throbbing hot seed of a herpes sore.

My God, I could hardly keep control of my body! I smiled stupidly and, ignoring her, turned to my work. I shoved the copier's buttons without effect, the machine somehow sensing my dread, refusing me. Maria came over. She poked at the copier once and it ran.

"Sure. Great," I said.

"Stu wants you in the TV room, he said for me to say."

"Yeah. I'm gone already," I said.

"No, he wants you 'now,' he said," she said.

"Wait. I meant like, *I'm there*. I'm gone . . . I'm going already."

"Huh?" She dabbed her nose with her wad of tissue, sniffling. "No, '*now*,' he said. Our commercial's on."

"Right, see?" I clumsily gathered my paperwork up as if done, piling thoughtless stacks. At the edge of things, I could sense something was smoldering, a fear coming. "But I meant it like, *'I'm going. I'm not even here, still,' see?*"

"No, not really."

I licked where my lips tasted hot from my herpes sore. "Wait a sec. Hold it a second," I winced.

Like my mother, Maria took hold of my shoulder, and I thought I would fall.

"Would it kill you for once to say 'yes'? Is that so tough? Or is it—is it just you *always, always, always* have to mess with me?" she said.

My voice sounded thin to me, and being almost a solid month single, I was unsure how to talk to her, or how to be. I just wanted to become tiny and to sleep again. I pretended to walk somewhere necessary, and rounding the corner to marketing I spotted our boss and the payroll guy, head-to-head. They laughed like conspirators, whispering things. Nervous sweat soaked me, beading up wet on my face and neck. I was sopped with it! I wiped at the sweat, but it wouldn't come off. Why pretend it would?

I hid. I knew I'd never make it until five.

I didn't know what was going on. For weeks, I had been waking and lying in my bed, still exhausted, denying the hideous white daylight that ruthlessly sucked me back into the world, me putting off opening my eyes again and fully returning to the land of the calm . . . my problems, my ex, Rebecca, tossing plates at me, me tossing them back. Truly, I didn't know what all was wrong. . . .

I had been having nightmares in which my stepfather beat me with his fists while I stabbed at him with a knife. Insane street people choking and embarrassing me. Dreams where I woke up crying, or muttering things, totally unable to remember what it was that I had just then, shivering, dreamed.

Now I hid with the ghosts of those 1970's bands in the stockroom—I should add that this was back when I worked the phone lines at Polydor during their last direct-marketing days, before we were mergered and swallowed whole. Sweet Melanie, Carly, and dull Helen Reddy. Hip-huggered Cher. I could almost reach out and touch her, there in the air. Through my window a floor-to-roof view of the city. We could all be free so quickly, I reasoned, troubled by these forgotten singers, and I leaned distractedly touching at myself in front of the other tiny office people who looked dazed in the building across from me. But below them, and down diagonally from me through my window, two snickering, suited guys stood silently waving up while a third man pointed for the unseen laughing others to hurry and take a look. And didn't this seem like it had all happened somehow before? Over and over and over again? No, not this specific humiliating incident, in the stockroom, but something uncannily like it. The onlookers always of course were different, yet more or less acted exactly the same.

I caught sight of the big, green FUJI FILM BLIMP careening then, trying to maneuver between our two buildings and appearing like some monstrous and absolute bomb, but hobbling, piggish almost, as if caught on a piece of string. The wind tugging it. Its pilots obviously drunk and almost fishtailing themselves into the towering lit-up Tishman building adrift in these skyscrapered winds. Beyond the green blimp rose a choir of granite spires, the knife-tipped Helmsley, the cakelike Plaza. *All of us*—everyone watching wished the thing would explode. What arrogance! What use was there even in trying in such a world?

I saw, outside and across from my building in a window a story or two down, another dress-suited, lonely worker. An older, unfortunate blonde woman in her own glass office who watched the blimp, or who had started watching it, and no longer actually was, as she thinly sighed. Then she touched her tears. I saw her! She was baring her heart—unaware and alone, with this unrehearsed act, standing angly there, nibbling the arms of her glasses . . . her suffering she just took for granted as part of our unending general despair.

You could read it all: she didn't still have a lover, that much was for sure. So what good was it? What use then were all of her objects, that shitty vase?

Britta, Rebecca, that blonde woman.

If only I could be there and touch her, I thought!

If only I could reach out and comfort her, whisper it, nuzzle those words in her hair.

I know you. I know where you're hurting, I said.

⬛

I thought if I could just come with her once. The doorknob unlatched and I crouched by a file of old disco hits. One of my sort-of friends, Leon, peeked the door open and slipped on in. "Beat me to it, man. Every day, someone's done sneaked here ahead of me." A handsome and Southern-voiced weightlifter, in a lousy band, Leon never seemed to much care.

"Whatever you're doing, you're caught," he said.

"What?" I said.

"God, you look horrible, buddy. No kidding."

"Pretty crappy, huh?"

"Kind of."

"I'm just feeling sort of like, well."

Leon closed us in. "So forget all this noise. What's outside? Hey, whoa," he said.

My eyes wrenched up, blurring with tears.

"Whoa, baby. You are *really* not feeling so good."

"Exactly, yeah. You've hit it right on the nose."

My mood flopped around like a tired child's, and

when Leon walked over to touch me, I flinched at this animal shine in his eyes, like a dog or something. I saw for a split second how he'd might like to bite me, to rip my throat, like everyone did on my morning train.

Leon crushed my arm. "Leave this shit. Let's go upstairs and let me buy you a beer."

"Our commercial's on. I've got to count when they air *Funk the World*." Our Polydor president, himself having a criminal cast of mind, did not trust that the regional television commercials he paid for would ever truly play as the stations said, so we each took turns for him counting their airings, we underlings, Leon, Maria, and me.

Leon flexed his neck muscles, and walnut sounds popped in his body. He tugged my arm. "Huh, say, you jerk off, let's split. Let's sneak upstairs to the bar for some beers."

"*What* was that?"

"What was when?"

"No, you said 'jerk off'. . . Never mind. Skip it. Well, first look if you see Maria."

"Maria."

"She hates me. She does!" I said.

He twirled the brown curls on his forehead. "No way, man. Might turn me like into a lizard."

"A toad, you mean."

"Toad, fucking rhino, whatever. See that big blimp up there? *We* got those doodads in Texas. For *Chuck E. Cheese.* I wonder, like, how would you. . . . What if you shot it?" he said.

—Something was wrong with my thinking. Our office girls, the blonde woman across from my window—if I could just hold her, or speak to her. It's not that I missed my old girlfriend. I missed all of them. I didn't trust anyone, but I couldn't bear being alone.

Once, I had tried to ask Maria to lunch, but my nerves failed me. Now I regret those unlived bits of life. And I ask myself—if only I'd talked to her, what would have eventually happened? Where would all of our rendezvous have led? To what secrets, what unrelieved hours of pleasure?

Leon and I headed for the elevator down at the service hall. We passed office doors. Desked workers wistfully glimpsing us, cloistered nuns, old guys erotically hopeless, yet each marked our passing, I thought, with that glance. Yes, it gripped my heart, everyone hiding their lives. We caught the big swaying elevator car to the bar at *The Top of the Sixes*. Leon clutched his crotch. "Don't let it get to you. I piss on that job from up here," he said.

What a cruel trick—that elevator! Inches away from my loafers, it fell away, the sheer, dropping black hole below us, so empty, that freon-cool, deep-shafted whistling air.

I felt queasy.

"Hey, I hope you're not broke," Leon said. Then a hundred floors.

Me, I suspected dark entities chewed through each cable's core. Grimy trolls, beings that squeezed from my consciousness. Yet if our elevator fell through the singing air, it would take only seconds to crush to our death.

Where would my girlfriend be then? I didn't know what was still eating me—my chest trembled. After our fight with the dishes, Rebecca made love to me down on our kitchen floor. She was bleeding, the linoleum petaled with thrown scrambled eggs. Making love to her, I thought we were maybe made up. We could talk it out. But weirdly, when I spoke to her, all I could make was this screechy slur.

—I was obsessing on women at work and projected these nervous and sex-filled imagined scenes, even now, shakily scouting the bar. Its chromey lounge. Another insanely high view of Manhattan. The place was dead. Leon knew our young actor waitress. They kissed hello, and she headed us off to a booth by the windows. Our first drinks were free.

Leon said, "That girl's Roberta. What a pair of lungs. Go ask who the other girl is, her barmaid friend."

"Are you kidding? Not me, man. I'm way too tense."

"Aw, come on, cheer up," he said.

I was helpless. There was nowhere to hide.

I looked down and away from the girls. I said, "I thought we were just sitting here, anyhow."

"We are," he said. "But we're in the catbird seat. . . . I think they've just finished their shift."

"No way," I said. "No! I'm not going."

"Okay, okay. All right already, then. If I'm not back quick, watch my drink," he said. Then he left, and I never saw Leon again.

I mean *ever* again. He was swallowed up.

While I waited around, hiding, my drinking arm shook like a starving pup, spilling gin and tipping my glass by the window. When I looked down upon our gray city, toy buildings, the miniature-golf-sized horizon reeled up tilting wrong like a carnival ride.

I threw back that blued icy gin.

It was nearly five, yet I couldn't cool down my mind.

○

Back at my desk hung this Post-it note left by Maria: —*You're dead,* it said. One the boss had signed read, *You are not here—4:10!* Then I heard Maria's cough come across our thin cubicles. Around me, a few office phones flashed on unanswered in a dozen dark offices and rang from the vacant desks. I was alone with her, trapped in our office. I knew I would see her before she arrived. In periphery, first her black dress, then the rest of her.

Major hips, cleavage, Italian lips. Maria dropped onto the swivel chair next to my ratty desk, and naturally, I glanced up her legs as she slumped, as she crossed her legs, and tried not to look up her dress.

"Guess what," she said. "Guess what I heard from the boss."

"Yeah, shoot," I said.

"You're up the river, I heard. To your neck in it."

"...Boy, that is *some* kind of dress."

She reached for her Post-it note, crumbling it up.

She was flaming. "A ten-year-old. . . . You done now! You finished, smart aleck?" she said.

I hadn't fully caught what I'd said. "What? What?" I said.

"My dress, huh."

I couldn't look at her straight in the eye and pretended I was staring at the doodled shapes scrawled on my desk blotter, panicking, my tongue feeling thick as clay. "*What?* It's nice!" I said, suddenly knowing some blush, or some gesture or muscular twitching, might somehow reveal to her I was afraid, *not of her*—but of all of the signs of my fear itself.

"You asshole. Is that all is left in your head? Christ, all you guys! Is *everything* sexual?" she said.

I looked at her shining black thicket of coiling hair. She leaned closer, until I felt where she breathed her cool breath on me. "What's up with you, Nim? You're wigging out. You're hitting on me—aren't you," she said.

"*Maybe.* Yeah," I said.

I didn't know what else to tell her. I couldn't see what to say. Every second, yes, God, what connivance, what lies! In between orders I AmExed, I had plotted the cloth-hidden arc of her breasts, and the rest of her. I imagined where her sex slanted up in her dress. I did that, the way that I do with all women. Every one of you. Only vaguely attached to my work. But now all the words muddled. I was caught. I couldn't see what to say. My pulse rushing, roared in my head like the Xerox. I just grinned at her, nothing inside me but air; that's it, I thought. Me, an inflated man.

Maria leaned over me, whispering, her arm sliding warm on my shoulder, her words buzzing. "Look, why don't we go out and talk somewhere." She touched my hair. "Is that what you're wanting? Are you trying to flirt with me, honey?" she said.

"I—got to run. I'm kind of nauseous," I said, unconnecting us.

"I'm holding you?"

I grabbed up my briefcase and jacket.

"Wait, hold the elevator! Let me go get my coat," she said after me.

I told myself, *not in a billion years*, punching the door button, and every other elevator button that would close the door. I wouldn't have made it alone in there, alone with her. Alone in the elevator's box with her mind.

I felt as if I'd been gnawed up inside of some giant mouth. Chewing sounds, everything wanting to eat.

What a nervous mess! Out in the canyons of city air, I dodged all the office-trons staggering for home. Exposed, it seemed, as if Maria had intruded into one of my dreams. No way could I secretly lust for her now, having ditched her, and now that I'd shown how I thought of her. Beneath Forty-second Street, I bought a paper to hide my face and caught an express for the Village. If I could just be off by myself, I thought, I'd be fine.

But dragging up from the stinking, dark steps of the subway I saw this small crack buzzard scamming on Twelfth Street, perched in a doorway, thin as death. I sped up some, automatically regretting I had done it, and slowed my walk almost to calm, but the thin dude had already moved out of his doorway. He scooted up, saying things, when he was hardly close enough to be heard, *"Sharp jacket, Slick. Say, let me ask you a question. Wait! Wait a second. Excuse me, goddamn you, a second,"* keeping by me, looking up with these wild navigational glances. *"Excuse me, wait! Shit, can't I ask you a question? You better'n me, Slicky?"* and such as that, a litany, like *I* had done something to *him*, I guess. Then he just snatches my arm like a crab.

"Whoa! What the hell? Jesus!" I said. What was going on? How did they sense when you'd weakened some? I couldn't ditch him, couldn't fend him off; he clutched at the sleeve of my jacket, and side by side, both of us broke into a jog.

Cabs honked and swerved from us.

Unbelieving, I pulled us out into the traffic, yanking free of him. *"Slick, look at here. You ain't together. . . ,"* he said.

I was running.

Near my neighborhood, one bum was bashing an older bum, throttling him. "Give me my dollar," the younger one yelled. The air had a color, like something was on fire somewhere. Things were starting to fog. Peripherally, the buildings were smeared with a nauseous blur. I had stood on this corner a zillion times, yet for a second I forgot where I was. I was all mixed up. "Give me half of one. Give me my dollar!" the younger bum begged.

I almost vomited.

Then things began jelling back, and I sensed my girlfriend, her essence, a few blocks away from my home. *I'm right here,* I said, and placed myself right where I was. I hid, and watched my apartment from beneath a thin dogwood tree. I was home now, but I couldn't go through the door, through that darkened hall. They could cut me down, strip me, and shovel my heart out; I didn't care. I couldn't talk anymore. My arguments with my girlfriend were waiting upstairs, not physically *her* with her actual body, but a memory-her. The aftershock of hours of fighting. Our anger, it pressed every inch of the walls. What tension! Our poisons would haunt up the air in there after Rebecca and I were long dead.

What else was it? I felt in my pockets, but I *still* couldn't find my damn keys. They'd deserted me. On the intercom, when I buzzed our drunk super to let me in, all I could make was that weepy slur. "Ruh," I said, "ruh, ruh, ruh."

I was so tired, with no chance to sit and be quiet somewhere.

So I flew off to Florida that evening on TWA, and I watched from the clouds with their angels as sad New York City grew small and dissolved.

. . . That blonde woman. If only I could be there and touch her, I thought. If only I could reach out and comfort her, whisper it, nuzzle those words in her hair.

At work one time, I heard this song playing, *Is that all there is to a fire?*

Bad Day

I had my problems. I got barely warmed.

I would never move back to New York.

Sure, a child wasn't dying. There were people in this world far worse off than me, and you could sit there, I guess, and honestly argue how I just wanted to feel someone's mothering pity. "Ah, cheer up," people said. I was really dumb. I thought I wanted to die.

This really happened.

Some months later, at Daytona Beach, hundreds of feet out in water, near the party pier, I floated about lazing in the aquamarine. Kind of treading time, neck-high in the glassy Atlantic. Pretty children, the beach sand, and toy-bright umbrellas. A lovely young woman waded wet from the surf. Saltwater lifted and filled, darkening, cresting around me and in my mouth as I bounced through a breaking wave. When the shark came, and shoved with the rubbery trunk of itself across my hollow belly, I thought that it felt like another wave. A fin caught me, scraping my ribs like a Frisbee, a horrible blurring sunk deep in the green. Some nurse shark or, who knows what—I didn't argue. I hopped myself up on that water. But it wouldn't stop. Its undersea, uncolored shape rubbed by me the length of a Chevrolet, and brushing by, pushed me as if to say,

Swim it! This is life. Swim, you idiot, swim. I was finally touched.

I'm like anyone.

I'm still scared, but I lived.

Immaculate

One night, this girl goes by her window toweling dry. She has a towel wrapped half around her and dabs some water off her back. I watch, but not at first on purpose. I see her dresser, a quilted bed, and a murdered mound of basket laundry. Then the girl comes back in dripping, when all I'm wanting to do is light a last cigarette off my stove.

She's sort of beautiful and chubby and tan as bread. She buffs her hair mussed up with one side of a towel, then folds the towel in half and dips her head to pat her wet hair with the dry side of the towel, the way you do, and I recognize it exactly. The dabbing and folding thing with the towel. The girl keeps patting at her hair, her naked neck and chest, her legs. I think, Oh wow. But God, she sees me, and I snap off my light.

Across the darkness, there is a seven-story drop between our opposite apartments, and sometimes window lights are on in other homes.

You see things. Take for instance the girl.

The truth is, I have glanced over here before at her, at night when I smoke in my kitchen. I've seen her messing around and distracted, inside her own life. Her secret head. She'll do anything, smell what she's clipped from her toenails. The normal things. Dark-haired, together, a business type. One night I saw her go out draped in pearls.

When she's dressing, her panties go on first, usually. But why is it her pearls are the last to come off?

So I'm out of work. Temping. I watch videos, thrillers and porn movies. Then I swear them off, praying to quit. Just like I've tried with these cigarettes. My clothes feel too tight and too nylony. I need a smoke. I can't sit still, then I see her.

I dig around, find a stale pack in the trash.

—She drops her towel and my heart starts

slamming, her rear to me, a cleft like some huge swell of fruit. The tan girl plops on the edge of her bed and combs the tangles from her hair. Back at my place, it is partially dark with the lights off, but my hands shake so much they look vibrating. They're as gray as smoke, or I see my hands windowed in silhouette.

Look at this—she bends to tug up a long white stocking. She yanks it off, and I try to light another cigarette on my stove.

I can't light it, though. Nothing works.

Like me, she's single. I figure she's getting herself dressed to go out again. A lonely girl, probably. I've seen girls like her sitting in bars with their married friends. And down the bar, men like me stiff with their beers, as if drinking lead.

Here is what she does: the girl goes digging through her dresser and finds white underpants and a large beige bra. She drops the wad of panties and belts the bra around her body. Kind of lifting up a breast, she shrugs. Then uncups her bra off and tosses it. She checks herself out in the mirror. She can't decide; maybe she'll just walk around naked. Her mind, I see, is thinking, but distractedly. . . three or four things at one time. She's pretty. She bends and her back makes a curved violin.

I know she can't hear me, but I move around quietly in my apartment. I hope that my place looks like any dark window. No one's home. I've gone out, she'll think. The burner on my stove is old, and only smolders the end of my cigarette.

I feel excited. I'm buzzing. The best so far.

Stay, I think.

My tan friend talks to herself now—she seems weepy. Beside herself. She sits on her bed, then gets up. She rummages in her dresser and finds another bra and hooks it on. As she sits, there's a healthy soft pillow of belly. It's sexy. The roundness looks right on her body, and her womb is there, over a glistening wet nest of brown hair. She could be pregnant, that shape, and I get hard as a rock. Now she acts impatient. She steps into blue jeans, throws on this big white billowy blouse, slips on some shoes, and leaves her room. *Kazam,* like that—I can't see where she's going, and her other rooms barely exist to me. She just leaves. I'm left. I stay.

I wait for her. I see her bedroom lamp is still burning.

Then she scoots back into the bedroom, knocking into things. She looks around the room, yanks up her loose, white, billowy blouse, and drags it bunched up over her shoulders. She tosses it. Below her place, another dim window light comes on. My friend drags clothes from her basket of dirty laundry and finds a slinky, black shirt with a V-neck and shakes the wrinkles from it once.

—Now this part is wonderful and perfect . . . my girl takes this shirt from her basket of dirty laundry, holds it loosely to her face, and *smells* the cloth. She breathes in it. Then she puts it on! Like the slinky, black shirt wasn't clean, but it's *clean enough*. It's sexier, shows the dark curves of her cleavage. The girl turns off her light. She's gone, while I sit here smoking alone in my kitchen, one last cigarette left in the pack.

The garbage pack. Carltons I stole from El Teddy's.

But outside, there are two or three other good windows. . . .

There's the one below, to the right of hers, where I watched a very old, wrinkled couple in their kitchen making love. Or at least they had been up to something just before I saw their light glare on. Whenever someone hits their light switch, I like watching that dust-filled bridge of light reach the wall to my apartment, as if you could walk across the light if you were small. Connecting us. Anyway, the woman there had to be seventy, and was *totally* gray. Her short, fat man could have been a beardless troll, his entire back mossy with hair.

This was back when I still had the job. I had cash to burn, no more stale smokes or dark windows.

I wasn't looking that night, but I saw.

—The old woman pranced in and heated a pan of water, while a cat hopped up on the countertop like it was mewing and mincing for food. Then that ancient guy sneaked in and hugged her from behind. He drew his hands down her wrinkled body, and he was moss there, too.

They both weren't pretty anymore. But it *still* was sex. She touched him. And how could that not affect you? Her skin was as naked as any young woman's. Her nipples were large and stiff and brown, and she was touching him that way. In silence. My God, they looked like something from the Bible. They were *too old*. He rubbed at her, and she turned—after putting the water on for their dinner, and she led him back to where these two had surely already been.

Immaculate

I light my last bad cigarette off the stove. A dry cough racks my chest like I'm dying. It fills my throat.

I say, "Okay, enough. Jesus . . . I'm quitting this shit. This is it."

Her upper window light comes on. My friend's other window lights up dimly. Here she is.

Her lamps and furniture and her quiet. She'd left, but now she's forgotten something, I'm thinking, and has come back into her home. I see her sulk in her long, shadowed hallway, heading this way. Her bedroom window light turns on. She yanks off her coat and the slinky, black V-neck and I have to catch myself, holding my breath.

She gets all the way down to her bra again, changing things, back to her baggy white shirt.

Now she's comfortable, finally—she's hidden her chest. This billowy shirt is more *her.*

I get up again, knocking about in my kitchen. Embarrassed for her. Hurting. It breaks your heart.

I swear I count six different changes of clothing, then she's back to the shirt, angel white, glowing like pearl.

I watch her bedroom light snap off. The hall light.

Now her place is dark. But a milky shape stands at her window. It leans away and floats back close to the glass. Her lights are off, yet she hasn't gone. She stands there glowing against the darkness. I don't know. Does she see me, I think? It could be she's not even looking out. Just being there, standing before her window in a kind of daze.

Then she comes to me over the darkness.

"Just this last one," I say. Just this once. How does it go?

And the devil, taking him up into a high mountain, showed him all the kingdoms of the world in a moment of time, and said unto him, If thou be the son of God, cast thyself down from here. For he shall give his angels charge over thee, to keep thee. World without end.

I unzip my pants. This is it, really, the last.

She's still herself, for now, in her bedroom. We are both ourselves. All of the windows are unlit. I wonder if she sees me. I wonder if she's watching the spark of my cigarette, off bobbing in the dark.

Cousins

My cousin Kay, thirteen and flirting, lets us look into her shirt front while we hoe our rows of corn. Kay leans, pretending she is innocent and bobs across from me; she weaves and wades through the flood of green on our weedy ground. On up the field our furrowed cullises of corn begin to merge, as if the knee-high rows of corn had zipped apart about her hoeing—blending overgrown in green again ahead. And farther still, the cornfield narrows, funneling row onto row to the end of our farm, where the trees are the edge of our world. We're Kay, my stepdad Lloyd, and Mama and Jim and me, and God.

It seems to me he's left us sweaty, hoeing useless at the earth. This thistled thorn-leaf spread of herb along the ground surrounds our corn, this burring beggarweed and horsetail, berried indigo and poke, the pulpy, lemon-petaled mustard, dandelion, wheaty cane.

Us in all-day sky and dirt, last year's pasture, this year's combed-in early corn. Dust. Summer's heat to come.

We're all so bored except for having her around.

Between the cornfield and the cattle field, we run the irrigation on our melons through the night, some forty automatic sprinklers. Dawn, an extra-thirsty cow will jump a fence to butt the pipes, to dash its muzzle in the water, gnaw a sprinkler's water stream.

We're in a tea bed thick of garden, sandy-bottomed, mostly weed. Kay and Jim hoe past on up the field. My mama and stepdad lagging, stand like scarecrows in their clothes, which rag with wind and flap their backs a dozen yards or so from me. Kay pulls her hoe out from the ground about the sucker stalks of corn. My cousin's hair falls from her neck. Beneath the skin, a string of nuts spine down her backbone in her shirt, which wraps in flannel wings around her, buttoned loosely at the front. Her hair reminds me then of boards. My brother, Jim, with Kay, says whispered

something, looks—if he were me—into her shirt
where Kay is shaded, paler her hid from the sun. Our
sunburned, blonde, and skinny girl.

She once let me chew her hair into my mouth like
wadded silk.

Jim does what I tried to do when I've hoed close to
Kay. On other weekends with my cousin I would talk
across the corn. We work on mornings when the crops
will drench our thin and soggy clothes. Her dampened
T-shirts fit her skin, her bent before me cutting squash
or tending laces on a shoe, her open shirt drapes in the
air. We watch her seashell-colored nipples on her body
while she hoes.

I mostly picture her remembered this one day, my
cousin over from our grandpa's house to help us in the
fields. My cousin's perfect branch of neck in yellow hair.

Sometimes her neck is like an animal alive inside of
her. Inside of Kay.

Dust shuffles in my shoes and wads my toes. Here
a row, here a weed, here a tug of hidy corn is buried
in the dirt. A tumblebug works scritching useless circles
in the dirt, little wars, its halves of back like lacquered
candy on the soft of it inside, two hooded wings to
shell its innards from the burning of the world. It rolls a

mealy, sculpted ball of turd, a boulder twice its size behind it, reared, intent, and kicking, freakish Atlas with its feet.

It wanders backward lost and blinded toward an ant-bed death to come. Me, I'm a giant to the bug. I wonder what its tiny mind is like, what nonsense it must live.

I kneel and listen at the world. I hear the gyroings and gears inside the belly of the world, oily and in tar— and in the sky, the set chain of the wider all—turns. No. I hear out here the wind. Work. Sun on us.

My cousin's fitty laughter purls a sound up in her mouth. The rippled leaves of little corn swish on our land. A breathing wind. Against the ground the air moves down to gently nudge the leaning corn in a changing green; the undersides of leaves wave shifting shades. Crockery green and olive. Unripe lime.

I dream of her. She showed her bruise to me in school. One time alone, when I was sick, I passed the gym hall doors that opened on the gym girls' locker room. I caught a glazed and dripping girl long in a towel, a sock in hand slides up a leg. Wet on a bench, the beaded backside of my cousin in a towel, the sound of shower waters on in a steamy light.

My stepdad fans his hat next to his head and scans the rows. "You all hold off and meet us up," my stepdad says to Kay and Jim. They catch a glance at one another, then look bothered back at me. Kay yawns—her mouth a bitten peach. Her open mouth hangs weighed with lip the way my cousin, tired, will. I'm nearly crazy watching Kay! She bends and lifts inside her shirt. She backward hoes my straggler's row of weedy field to meet us up.

"Find any corn in these here weeds?" she says.

"I lost my shoes," says Jim. "I can't believe there's not a tractor what can't do this kind of work."

My stepdad's face. The way he stands says things to us that he does not say.

"All right. Well, I'll just do the rest," he says. "You plugs go on inside."

"Now, Lloyd, they're fooling," Mama says.

"It's good they got their sense of humor."

"Lloyd, I swear."

My stepdad plants his hoe and goes to check the sprinkler lines.

The podded weeds will live the longest, taller corn dry paper-leafed, the sandy ground turn clay and shatter. Calves will die.

A rusty nail lies bent and petrified with ruin, limbs

of twig, pebbles, sand in barren canyons, tiny-sized.
I'm daydream gone, lost in my head down at the small,
this anted world. Some days I'm not much good at
work; I'm pretty worthless, usually gone. My bug rolls
through the ants stirred in a penny-colored boil.

I don't see how God could think of everything at
once, each nothing twig and little desert.

I think God has turned his back on all us bugs.

When we knock off to miss the sun we are a circus in
our lunch amongst the hay bales and the siloed high
baskets stacked like cups out in the open, airy shed, a
shed cleared empty save the hay bales, seed, and tractor
in a hulk. Lunch is paper sacks: our coiny Necco
Wafers, sandwiches, potato chips, and Cokes, orange
and grape and nut-float sodas. Nuts float in the soda
neck so they're already wet each time I tilt my Coke
to sip, so cold and fizzing, munchy foam.

Mama has her cigarette and figures on the basket
slats some crayoned days and numbers. Lloyd on a
basket at his sandwich seeks an outer something hazy
on our farm, jawing sideways balls of lunch.

It hardly seems like God could really care.

Here are Mama and Lloyd with drinks and me in tossed electric shadows of our television's glare. Kay lies on her elbows on our living room floor. TV news. My stepdad swirls the ice cubes in his glass, says, "That's it," says, "Bright-eyed and bushy-tailed," and gets up. Now it's the Late Show movie on TV.

Mama says her shoo-on-you's—her voice a kind of horn. Says, "Just a second minute. I just want to see the start. I heard about this one; it's a good picture. It was good when it was a movie, still."

Lloyd swats her leg with folded news. "Let's get to bed, woman. You're not watching no scary picture. You'll be fighting boogers all night long."

"Oh poo. You wish."

"Let's hit it, Mom."

"I got to hug good night my lambs."

She hugs. Her smell gets on my head.

Kay slowly curls onto her back dressed in my mama's borrowed wrapper. Lacey roses red on pink and sleeving drawn along her legs, the trim unraveling in loose ends of its fishing line thread. My cousin puts a finger to her teeth and bites the nail;

she is a grinning blonde to Lloyd while he tongues his smaller ice.

Kay is the only living girl like her around. Out here there's mostly trash and cattle, burnt-up orange trees and corn, the Yankee trailer houses scattered, colored shacks. We've got our church on up the road, a Stuckey's, Grandpa and Grandma's tin-roofed house, the store at Cuchard's Gulf. The farms, and cattle dotting pastures. Empty fields.

A steady night-slush sound of semis on the four-lane miles away.

Some nights I'll walk off in the dark to watch the headlights' tracing beams, the faces floodlit on the billboards in the night. Driving. People in their cars I'll never know.

Lloyd switches off the lamp. "You all don't make no noise," he says. "Let's keep it to a whimper." Lloyd peers at our TV as if he pays no great attention to my cousin in her sprawl, her lying laid out like the wounded on our oval, banded rug.

Out past the curtains on the window, brightened moonwash frosts our lawn. I try my bumbling look of interest in the same old picture tube. My stepdad winks at me and goes.

Mama says, "Now just this one," and then for me to go to sleep. "It's a weekend's worth of weeding, boy, before you've got your school." She says this with a face like mine the way she sometimes is, my mama's face awake and haloed and her hair teased up for bed.

Alone, I'll try to do her smile and make myself turn into her, me smiling, dolled up in the mirror with her lipstick slid on me.

I'll kiss her cool and mirrored image. Leave a lip print red with wax.

"Don't be up late, you two," she says.

Mama and Lloyd in the bathroom turn the bathtub water on, their voices boinging on the water. Water sloshes, muffled noise. When the water stops I hear my mama mutter something, me and Kay, and something other, Jim and Nim, like everything she says to Lloyd has somehow to do with me. I see their legs locked in the water and their places dark with hair, my mama straddling my stepdad, then the shower. Water sounds.

Him naked, hairy in the water on my mama coupled-up.

I see her furred and fitting skin.

Him coupling Mama in the water as her face turns into mine, with Mama bent into the shower water,

111

naked, *me as her*. To hear their talk, my cousin fidgets
with the TV volume knob. We get my mama's lilting
questions, scooted seat noise from the john. I nudge my
cousin where she lies down on the floor between my
feet. Then Lloyd follows Mama to their room and shuts
the door; their tabled bed lamp switch is clicked. Their
closet hangers softly ding. Kay shrugs her shoulders at
my toes. "You best behave yourself," she says. "I'll put
a hurting on your butt."

She sort of sings into these words so I will guess
that she is playing: Kay is happy we're alone. I know she
is. Our wooden house's hollow dark draws in to watch
us in the room. We've gotten bigger in the room since
they have gone. Our bodies—mine, at least, feels
better-looking, rubbery, and strong. I feel like I'm not
such a kid.

The light thrown from our television moves in
shifting blues and grays and whitish paths of light, the
dark and lighter colors shadow us. My cousin rests her
head upon her elbow on the rug. She tugs her wrapper
up a bit to scratch some pink into a knee; she bares her
powder-whitened leg, the wrapper riding on a thigh.
She smooths the fabric to her skin. Her spooning rear is

woman-bigger than the rest of small girl her. My cousin sighs a shallow yawn.

"It's getting I can't raise my head," she says.

"Yeah, girl, but don't I know."

Kay scratches reaching at her back as if a crab is in her hand, as if a crab had left its husk and inched with fingered, meaty claws. "Feel at this knot on me," she says.

Afraid of her, I nod my head. I sit here foolish on the sofa, sort of stiffened, mostly pose. I'm mostly bones and hands and legs. A churning curdles in my stomach, eases shuddery to calm. I get the fear and then it goes. I make a hard-on watching Kay. I put my mind inside the girl; inside of her, *inside her body*, I imagine all the colors in the hollowness of her, the tubing pipework of her blood, her netted stomach gourd in gray. The veining blue, her corded red. Branched through the organs dark in Kay, the beading cauliflower tree of clabbered, milky-yellow eggs. The stuff in her! And the hollower dark of where Kay is a girl and the wet-bag, girl guts of her. My mind lets pictures of the hair, like on my brother, cover Kay. I put a knob like his on her, and underneath my brother's thing, I put her lipped and pinkish hole. A slit, he says. A tongue in teeth between her legs, a mouth in fur.

Her skin pretended in my head.

I see my cousin in the shower with my brother over her. Kay takes the television's lighting on the rug. She bends a leg across her other one, her place up in her panties, banding low about her hips. Where she has shaved, the peppered skin. She has her heart and lungs inside of her in darkness in her chest, and air is there somewhere as well, the liquid ball of light in Kay, and Jesus' face is in her, too. I stretch out my foot again and nudge her with my toe.

This is how I picture her: my foot warm in her hair.

"You having fun?" my cousin says.

A sort of dare.

I feel a shiver shrink an inch of me; I drop my silly leg. This is the sign from her to move. She tilts her head to show her collar's downy blonde. She has these vacuum-hosey rings around her throat where I could hold, where I could pull her hosey throat from her—or put her in my mouth and bite it sucking from her head.

Across the television, talky, people wander on the tube.

My cousin curves into the places pressing Kay against her clothes. I touch the nutting of her spine. I tell her, "Goll, you're knotted sore."

I'm not afraid of her, I swear.

"More near my head," my cousin says.

"Is it like here?"

"Hold at my thumb."

She shows me where.

"Rub at this muscle, Nim?" she says.

⸻

Kay stills unnormal on our floor. We are the warm that is the air; a something back and forth between us running airy, kind of hums. The air, it jitters cues from Kay to me—and back from me, to her, like she knows what is doing in my head to do with her. My hard-on frog goes soft, then filled again, as I am rubbing Kay. This girl could float up like a bird or like a puppet in the air down on our late show, Kay-sprawled, living room floor.

My fingers slip into an armpit damp in stiff and twirling curls. I get her powdered, biscuit smell. She holds my wrist against her shoulder like a hoe within her grip. She drags my hand across her skin, across the deep and heated pocket of her collar's bony ridge. Kay tinted dimly on our floor with my hand on her shoulder, says a word; she whispers almost–all–a–word, or Kay, her throat, it sort of loosens on her air breathed into her. My cousin breathes a whispered no. "That feels like butter, there," she says. Inside my underwear the buzz. Here in the warm tucked in her clothes my fingers trip across the bumping of a barely risen mole. I feel the plumping where her chest has swollen ulcerous from her. Her breast is swollen as a bruise. Surprised, and not all that surprised, I'm disappointed that it's real. I feel this damp and nippled leaf around it, Kay, her flimsy pea.

The cooler night outside our house has settled; boards begin to tick. Out in the window stars and satellites and planets bite the sky. There's not a soul up in the world.

"We better not," is what she says.

My cousin looks at me. We kiss.

I don't care for her a second. Well, it's true.

My cousin sits up from the floor and turns the side of her to me. She lets her clothes fall down her arm a bit, her shoulder skin a little and the sunblush on her neck. "I'll pull this down some, if you want," she says, and folds along my arm. She holds her fingers to my palm and draws me close to show me more. Her dark below her tented belly in the warm within her clothes. I see the fur.

"You like my chest enough?" she says. "You want a touch?" Kay rests her head against my legs and leans herself where we can see. Her hill of breast against her slip. Her thin and mushroom-looking nipple darkens television blue. Her on my mouth, her in my hand. I cup her breast as if my cousin bulbed with water in her skin. She rests her head between my legs. I feel her press herself to me, feel where the water runs cold through my hands to my sides in the cold air pipe of my shirt into me, and the shower room cold starts to freeze where I am, where the water shrinks me in our gym.

But I am not afraid of her.

I am not afraid of her.

I am not afraid of a girl.

My brother boot-toes through the door. He's home—and my brother at our door sees my hands on the girl and the blur of my hands from her clothes. He glances leery at the girl—Jim grins at me, his raccoon face a mask of tractor soot, and his boots in their dust give a kick at our door while my brother sees me over her. My brother sees Kay in the blue on our floor.

"It's time you got to bed," he says.

So I wash and go to bed.

I hear our living room crick when I wake in my room, and the grunts are a girl and my brother, Jim's, wind, and the sounds of the world are of Jim and of Kay, when our girl on our farm in the whole wide world is the sound of my brother on her.

Another Sunday afternoon, our normal nothing weekend sunny day of sky. Outside, the weeds stressed in the wind begin to tremble, fiery, in green the germing puff of dandelions, nightshade, wheaty cane. We are at our hoes in the sun where the rows seem to blend, then to wedge at the fence with the trees in a line like a hedge.

Across the field my stepdad yanks a lane of irrigation pipe, he straightens, walks a length of pipe, he bends again. We hoe the corn. My mama and brother and leaning Kay. This year the heat is early in on us. The burning blades of corn wilt twisted mouse tails at their ends; some weeds in bloom lose all their petals, budded yellow flecks the ground, the crickets, blackflies, ants and beetles, speckled lace-winged ladybugs.

When Lloyd finishes the pipes, he turns the irrigation on, the spouting fountainheads of sprinklers sputter water, pelting beads.

"You all come get a drink," he says.

We plant our hoes and come. We kneel and drink beside the water, wash our faces in the water, wet our heads. Kay goes to stand into a stream. Before the sprinkler's circled course my cousin braces in the spray. A glassy shatter showers her. Our water darkens through her clothes and soaks the whiteness from her hair. A pond of water fills her smile, the push of waters denting Kay—a misted, water headache haze surrounds the girl. I put inside her what I see, our house, our barns, our fields and cows. Our cantaloupes and melons wait in garden rows for rain where the sprinklers churn.

This weevil fidgets with a flower till I crush the tiny life of it beneath my sneakered feet.

I don't hate her all that much.

I wonder, why does God let Jim have her . . . and not me?

I've seen a sow eat half its farrow. All our egg yolks

break in red, all bloodshot, fertilized and veiny with our rooster's useless seed. Unborn. We scrambled up those suckers, so then, why should I be kind? I call the dust bowl sandy drought on us, a plague of locust, fire, on my brother down from God.

The Living
and the Dead

—for J. C.

If only you were with me. If only I could show you his rusted old city, with the red brick trembling and the domed Vatican basilicas on fire, the sun over us like God. I bummed a cigarette, sitting there sleepless among a cheap scatter of papal cafés waiting for some guy who wouldn't want to have *anything*, I knew, to do with me, considering how poor and unblessed I was. I was all but broke. I wasn't like anyone I'd ever known.

The night before, I had slept hiding in the dim amphitheater of Verona, another one of those crumbling coliseums where blood had been poured to amuse the town for hundreds of years on the earth, and wherever I settled, I dreamed on that mortared-up, narrow, brick staircase, of someone stabbing me. Repeatedly—I mean I dreamed this dream over and over, of my being ripped open while I slept right there where I was. I was still learning to believe in my sense of things, and dreams like this happened wherever I went.

But now all around me were obvious pairs of young men. Bored Romans, at canopied, dim cafés. *Cinzano*, and words like that, throbbed at the cafés from lozenge-shaped bright metal signs, on each awning, like the neon-lit beer signs in windows in bars back home. *Jaco Bacci. Pellegrino.* Italian words. I missed home.

I had dropped out from Hunter, and for over two years I'd been bumming around train stations, tourist sights, hitchhiking with Deadheads and hostel trash. Permanent student-type loafers. A horde of us drifted across Europe. In Norway we worked a few weeks in the canneries. We'd pick fruit for a while. When it got cool on the beach we would pool our funds or sleaze off the rich Swedish tourist guys, anything to drum up a place to stay. Then it was fall again, and I knew it was too cold to sleep out for long, but I had to hitch off on my own.

I was young, though, and if I found a shower I could

still look okay. Unlike most everything else in the Vatican, the men's was free, so I slicked my wet hair back and brushed my teeth. I called Luciano, this stranger, while faking a normal-guy voice on the telephone, deepening it. I needed to get out of the cold.

"Ah, no. I mean, actually—I'm a friend of a friend," I said.

"Como, eh? What is that, friendy friend?"

"—Of Eddie's, the bar waiter."

"Eduardo, yes?"

"Eddie, right, the waiter in that muddy-floor café in Venice?"

"Yes, I know. *Edy*, Eduardo. Is no difference."

Luc said he would meet me and map out his town.

Amazing, was that how it always had worked? Thin beings, incredibly fine-bodied creatures looked out for me, haunting my air like a mist.

—I lied that I'd just left a really nice hostel, but most nights I spent sleeping curled up outside churches, and in cruddy fields, in public parks, car lots, the Parthenon. In such countries, I didn't have to show who I was if I didn't want to. I didn't have to please anyone for days.

A thin young guy walked from the Vatican porticos, kind of looking around. Then he saw me nod. One of those shirts made of linen or silk. We shook hands like two businessmen and I caught that glance where you kind of just know. Like an idiot I told Luc that he must be *him*. And what can I honestly tell you? His face, I mean. Beautiful. I could have cried.

"But you are not him," said Luc, chewing his lip and sitting next to me. "On the telephone I expected some other type . . . not like you. A big, smiling, you know, *American*."

"You were thinking some big, dumb American clod?"

"Yes! Only—how we say. A cap on, and holding this hamburger bag."

"A tourist, you mean. Sure, that's all right. That's okay. After all, you don't look that much Italian." The truth was, Luc looked like me, with these underfed, penitent features, a looseness, the same spiky, dirty blond hair.

Luc said his father was from Varanasi. "An Indio. My mother's of Italia and Suisse. Me, I'm everything. And you?" he said.

"I'm nothing, I guess," I said.

124

"By yourself," he said. "Just is you."

He was shimmering, and I was so nervous I barely could follow a word he said. My ouzo glass puddled wet rings on our table. He touched at it and drew faces in the water with his fingers, then he laughed at me.

"Hey, what are you laughing for?"

"It's just that you look so . . . oh. *Gatolino*, eh? How should I say in *American*? Like this skinny cat."

"Fuck you," I said. "I can go anywhere I want in the world. My arms are strong. I'm picking olives next Monday in Palma."

"Don't have a *fit*," he said. "It's good you are able to just . . . travel. I'm not so brave. Anyways, I don't know what I should explain you, or where you should go. It's weird, no? To meet like this? And also, well. Look at me, *basta*. Now I'm getting shy."

He crossed his arms trying to look tough. He was blushing. I wanted to reach out and touch him. He could loan me clothes, maybe even give me a sweater.

I'd been burned by this kind. Little wives. You get promises, then catch them out sleeping with half your friends, gym teachers, bartenders, anyone.

I leaned to him, staring at his chest again. "Well, I don't want to get in your hair," I said.

"My hair?" he said. "Yes, sure, of course. I'm so busy, see. . . ."

"Okay, then, you want an ouzo or something?"

He gave me the look. Luc flapped air up his shirt so it floated across him and fell like a sheet. What a mix of genes! His arms were like pale terra-cotta. "No, Hindus can't drink this. Oh, what the hell, a little, with water," he said, and his face sort of brightened to signal our waiter. *"Duo Pernod."*

A tall waiter boy brought us our cocktails and dropped the check. I fumbled around counting my last several lira.

"Please," he said, "I'll get these," palming back two of my small-looking bills. His chest was tan. In Europe, fags sunned on nude beaches, where I often slept. The waiter boy watched us, but I looked down Luc's shirt as he searched for cash, his underarm glistening dark, thick with tobacco-brown hair. I wanted to lick off his skinny, young body.

He had seen me stare. "Well, well, well," he said. "I'll let you walk with me."

"Sure, why not. You're not so ugly," I said.

"Oh, really, eh? You don't even *live* somewhere, sweety," he said.

I was messing it up. To speak as an equal like this was confusing me, as until then, I'd been meeting people only inside of their cars, hitching pointlessly. They were all nervous . . . and I never quite saw what they wanted from me. What they never said. Still, they were always in charge.

We walked down the cobblestoned Vatican plaza and strolled a stone bridge to the Tiber bank, lingering by tarnished green sculptures, a crowned Jupiter, a turquoised Poseidon, then another square. Everywhere ancient dead, haunted time. Anisette, the smell of burnt coffee and cigarettes. All I could think of was touching him. His skin was warm and ocher in sunlight. Tanned Roman men would come up and say hi to him. They'd nod to me, everyone kissy and smiling.

But I was exhausted now. I saw my reflection bend out in a window. It looked all wrong. My clothes were worn out and my hair was wrecked. He looked great. My heel caught a cobblestone, and for a second I thought Luc wanted to say something.

". . . It's fine," I said. "Let's go on."

"But maybe the shoes is broke."

"No, it's fine," I said.

"Okay, sure."

"Look. Really. It's fine now! Forget it." I tried to walk where the heel wouldn't make a loud scritch. I hated how hip foreigners would parrot the weird ways you could talk, *"Okay sure. Piss off. Forget it."*

Then evening came. Luc dug a pen from his pants as we sat on the wall of the fountain Navona. I slumped emptily, all worn out. I was going to talk, but being seen so much was starting my panic up.

"The day's all gone, isn't it? Listen . . ." Luc asked me. He patted his mouth as if thinking, and pursed his lips. ". . . Why I'm hanging around? You haven't came here to see *me*. You want now that I should just go away, leave you alone in the city? You are traveling. Afterwards, *buh*? Who knows? Maybe you come see me before you go."

Then they're gone like that. Every time.

Luc leaned back a bit cooling and distant. I touched just the tips of his fingers.

At my feet lay an uncrushed and perfect white cigarette, and of course, I thought, *I could pick it up*, or come back whenever he left. I let his fingers go. Women looked.

"Hey," I said. "Maybe, sure, I'm like . . . whatever." I hated this part when you met them, their kissing off, and the acting like you couldn't care less.

Leave, leave! I thought.

"It's too much," he said. "What's the phrase? I don't just party, and that, like for sport."

We stood numbly looking around by the fountain, at wet Neptune. On the cobblestone a child tossing rocks at some pigeons, which flitted up stupidly, then settled back inches from where they'd been.

I wondered, if only I could ask him to stay. I said nothing though. He shook my hand. A blind man could see I was sad.

"So, we are lucky then? In the piazza today, we may have looked and just missed ourselves. Karma, no? How did we know who the other one was?"

I kissed his head. "Yeah, spooky," I said, and he left. This wasn't only lust. It wasn't the way he talked; it wasn't his chest moving under his gauzy shirt, but something else, which neither one of us ever said.

—But you think I'm claiming I'm some kind of worldly prince, when, in truth, I never knew fuck-all about where I was. Or what I would sleaze my way into that night. And I didn't know Europe any better than America. This could have been anywhere,

Lauderdale, Venice Beach. I still wouldn't have had a clue.

For months I'd been stuck between rides on the highway, and a cloudy film hung between me and the world, some barrier, while the rich were so close, and the prosperous would glare from their vehicles, their restaurants, as if dirtiness, say, or my funky smell would sicken whoever came near—just like I'd treat some poor derelict.

And I ask you, who the fuck are you? How do you think you are so immune?

Now my teeth hurt, my shoes were loud, and I didn't have the money to get back to America. But where would I have gone if I did? I couldn't sponge off my destitute mother. My ex-lovers were heels, all of them. The days were still warm. Though at night it could drop down and freeze your toes, waking you up in a pool of ice. I knew I needed to get off the road.

Some days earlier, as I hitched down from Bonn at the overpass, soaked with sweat, a brilliant Mercedes moaned under the bridge. The man checked me out and nodded for me to get in. His head silvering, a man you might see in those magazine ads, in a paneled room ambered with fire. We drove on in silence for over an hour, in luxury. His air conditioning cooling my sweat. The autumn plain dryly bleeding up its last greenness. Bavaria. The straw-colored Saarbrücken meadows.

The man put on sunglasses.

"You see," he said, suddenly, as if dreaming back, fogged half-asleep in a lecture, "we are now owning *totally everything*, even you. . . . A commission of strong internationalists, British oil, Rotheschildes, Mushita, the Krupps. This is nothing new. Your leaders all know we exist. Hell, they are often us." He turned his wrist baring the palm.

So he told his tale, picking it up where he'd left the thread. German dials, a leathered and woody interior. What a life this man had to have led, in his haloed light. Sometimes you would think they were angels, the very rich.

"—And the ancient East? The East we carved up like an auction block. Bidding went on as with cards, huh? Vacant lots . . . millions of poor little fools."

Yes, he thrilled me, as he nipped now and then from a plastic cup swearing this rap was the plain holy truth, with its tentacles. Sure, he had lost his soul, but he once in a while had to tell someone, a human face, a powerless, small nonentity. And afterward he drove for a ways before asking me, even me! Wasn't I tired of driving and wouldn't I like maybe having some gold?

What they never said. But sometimes the both of you knew.

I couldn't though.

The earth listened.

I wasn't happy, yet I never was bored being alone.

It was horrible finding out I wasn't perfect, or anywhere even near to being perfect—and if I'd *had* a home I'd have left it then. I was hiding from people knowing how much a jerk I was. People found me, though, anywhere I ever went.

Now I just slept where Luc left me alone with that cigarette, going nowhere much. Oh, fuck it, I told myself. If things went bad I could just split. If he messed with me.

Luc lived upstairs in an ancient, red, stuccoed apartment, on a narrow street. I pulled the knobbed wire that rang his door. We were still awkward. The furniture was all velvet, and I couldn't figure out where to sit myself. I hadn't yet kissed his mouth. He led me around his apartment, my hands twitching. His books were huge. None of the usual dumb kitsch. There were posters of flaming, nude demons, the Indian gods. Embroidered divinities bannered his living room. Incense. I flipped through his old Hindu texts. "And this one, here?"

He eased to the couch and sat next to me.

"*Dakini*. The manifestation of female. Her energies."

An elegant god crowned in stone fire.

"... He is *Siva*, the power of male, the destroyer."

We read, leaning. What I wanted was to pick him up over my shoulders and put his whole body inside my mouth. He was so right. As he'd turn the page, reading strange names in their Sanskrit, he knew I kept looking up into his hair, and it pulled me in.

—I was pathetic. I could only feel whole when I loved. Then I'd crumble up.

Luc stood hugging a book. He said, "Why don't you stay a few days?" He would show me things. I lied that I would find somewhere cheap near Tresteverre. I told him I didn't want to get in his hair.

"Oh, that's stupid. The gypsies will eat you alive," he said. "I think you don't have so much money.

While me—I have. Besides that, we can just, as you say, 'hang around.' "

I told myself, Jesus, just do this and save your skin. My feet were shot, but I couldn't bear hanging around being pleasant, being on so much. The way that my mother had been, pretending to sing to herself from the radio, or drunk with Dad—comatose, the two of them covering things over with quiet. I'd never live life like them. He would wreck the place, beat her up. *"Look what your mother's caused now,"* he'd said.

Then Luc bought me dinner and got wine for us, cigarettes. We fixed me a place on his couch, and he said good night. We were like virgin queens. We didn't know what else to do, though maybe our spirits rose up from our bodies and met on the tiles of his hallway, where we'd couple up. I just lay in the dark in his living room, sneaking wine, safe and all dry with real pillows. I was gone somewhere, there in a house of the Romans. I was damp with sweat, and I touched myself, making him up in my covers, imagining him. Tomorrow. *Domani.* I almost came.

"Rick," his voice lulled from the darkness, his bedroom. "You are *still* awake? You don't have to sleep there," he said.

In his bedroom, I sat on the bed with the lights off. Still and obvious, trembling inside like a teenager. He raised himself, the sheet glowing blue as he held it. We were still a second. His face bluely windowed and nightlit. Then he rolled in dim bedsheets to kiss me, his layered ribs, crushing the sheets to his belly. The dark oval nipples, his neck. His lips were dry. He closed his eyes; his tongue like some small dampened offering. We kissed like that. My shirt came off . . . and I could describe our small gestures, that erotic buzz, and how it was having our chests touch, our pressing—but how could you feel it, or even see? "These pants," he said.

I kissed his skin, feeling him grip me, and all down my spine and along my cock, a heat warmed me. The brilliant light flooding my body. *This is me,* I thought.

A cat meowed somewhere outside.

"Eh, cosa vuoi?" Luc pulled his arms from me and slipped off, paled into darkness. I heard water, then a board of light swept from his kitchen and he padded back in with a bottle of wine. "I wanted you soon as I saw you," he said.

"Oh, sure," I said. "Then why did you ditch me?"

"Eh?"

"Nothing," I said.

135

We lay drinking, when I felt that bad feeling again. Then I saw the thing blurring up out of the dimness, a horned thing resembling a monster pig. A window-sized, Hindu god tapestry.

"—Shit," I said, "you don't pray to that ugly old thing?"

"You are thinking he's Satan. *Il diablo*, no?"

"Hey, whoa," I said. I knew that evil could come if you said its name. I could feel it there, and my anger welled up as if chemically.

Luc kissed me.

A cat started yowling outside, then it wandered off.

Luc turned his long body in moonlight. His ass in the air, with his swelling immaculate chest, the hard knots of his ribs and his stomach, then more of him, a ghost-colored waist in the dark. He leaned over and drew me up into his lips. I was full of light, sunk to someplace without color. We were gone somewhere. Now in a house of the Romans. Then he made me come. When we rested, he drank the wine straight from the bottle, his mouth pursing, and squirted the wet on our bodies. My God, I thought, *this is me*. This is where someone could find me.

I was really saved.

"*Che bello*, you still have these socks on," he said. He held my foot. "Maybe we'll buy you some new."

"And in exchange . . . let me guess. I'm to do specifically what?"

"Now you get it, eh. That's it, 'specifically what.' "

Out on those frozen roads, did I mention how most nights I slept with my shoes on or pillowed them under my head? Each night I was more of a nervous hysteric than the day before. Conversations, and elaborately mystical dramas flooded up from me, like those devils hung up in Luc's bedroom—or my father, for instance. He saw himself as always the victim and believed that the hard, *insentient* things—nuts and bolts, motors, the concrete and mechanical objects of everyday reality, were conspiring against him. I'd see him frustrated, trying to loosen some nut or something, and then whip around hitting at it, over and over again with his hammer, at our blender, say, and beat it as if trying to kill the thing. *"Well, kiss my ass! See what you motherfucking get,"* then he'd throw down the hammer and walk away.

". . . That's enough. To hell with the suck-ass bitch. Skip it."

Alone like that, things become real in your brain. Or they did with me. Back at Hunter, it had gotten to where walking through a classroom in which people were just hanging around talking required a sense of inner calm, a self-esteem, which totally eluded my grasp. I had been losing jobs, unable to breathe in an office—I was too scared in all honesty to tell my friends, or anyone, just how afraid I was. I would keep my old coat on and sit by the doors. Like my mother, Floridita, and the way she would stare out her window pressed up to the passenger's side of our car. I rode like that. One night they fought and he pushed her out. I saw her fall. I watched her blow out through her car door, and I heard as her clothes flapped like birds at the grass.

I just floated out, penniless. Who knows why? I'd been traveling. Then finally I got somewhere clear.

After riding that night with the Mercedes man, I left his nice car for a semi truck, and later was stranded somehow by the Autobahn out in a humid and cloud-covered pasture. Dark as some absolute basement of night. The next town was a Teutonic village dropped off on the farthest black edge of the world. Vibration, and the truck's roar bored through my body still. God, I thought. Typical. I'll just walk out and sleep in this field, and I crossed a ditch. It was like lowering myself down a blackened well. Yet I knew I wasn't all by myself. I sensed something haunting here, spirits, a consciousness. So totally blind as I groped around, I could feel what must always be with us. Dark figures. Things seemed to be breathing right in front of my eyebrows—almost brushing me, and I shuffled, exhausted, way off from the road. I lay down and slept.

But I woke in mud. To a milk-white, hideous lightning I thought was a dream. It was raining. I had sunk or the ground had risen up to surround me, and all my stuff, and I slapped out reaching through muddy pools. Blackness, a freezing and locustlike rain. I glanced around whenever the lightning flashed, and when the sky lit up grayly I could see to move, but the ground had gone from being an empty field into a muddle of rain-flooded sewers. The lightning hit. Out in front of me, a fence with white posts like a photograph negative netted a field of black hills, and I stumbled until I felt the fence guiding me. Buzzing, its cold wire sang like another mind. Then oddly, right above me, a paleness wobbled over the earth, showing violet clouds, and my teeth tasted funny as pennies, electrical, and a moon-white, thick trunk of light leapt my fence line and angrily whacked at the sky, while the shotgun noise *banged* in my eardrums, and I could hear fence wire popping like couch springs and raking the air. When I tried to run, my foot held as if something were grabbing me, had clutched my boot, a hand, a root, something, and like anyone I thought it was ghost people. Murderous men, grizzly dead soldiers crawled rotting from death who were pulling me back in the mud—I could see their heads, shapes I could sense in the darkness, but I jerked from that boot like it boiled!

Incredible. I felt that whole wonderful heart rush from missing the lightning and not being dead. Like clean oxygen. I felt all washed and alive.

I was ecstatic, but there was no one around I could share this with. My heart singing, hugging the neck of pure terror. I reached back there, but my boot was swallowed up in the earth, and it struck me at that moment that I'd surely wandered off in some grave-yard, as it lightninged blue. Big slabs of concrete like sewer lids. So I pulled off my other boot, and ran and fell. But where would I have run if I could? I was sure

I could sense the lost souls in this plot of ground. And what had been.

—I felt lit up inside.

Every time! Soon enough people would steal them, or you'd freak out and run off and lose your nice shoes. In a muddy field. Alone like that, *you* could have, too.

I started to trust in my sense of things. Not then, but later, looking back at the Hammond map. Yes, I swear. Historic deeds figured in that real estate, *final* things. A hallowed ground. That's all I'll say.

After that, I headed off hitching for Rome.

—And sometimes it's hard to believe that they're all the same stars. The ones outside my window, and the stars that were over my head back then on those empty, ghosted roads.

So I settled in. *You still have these socks on,* he said.

Luc got me things: sunglasses, Levis, a new pair of suede Pappo Gallos. I would sweep and pick up when he left. You get used to it. For weeks we just wandered his city, through the Coliseum, to the huge sculpted fountains, or whatever all, and Luc had to stop us and touch me. Every hundred feet, stopping to hug in the shade of things. Underneath columns and viaducts. In ruins. By the tremendous exhaustions all awaiting collapse, or we would lie in his bed and make love. It was all we did.

But at least I could trust that he wasn't out sleazing. Luc would be hanging all over me—he inhaled my breath.

Then autumn blew in at us, and maybe he sensed I'd get bored and leave; he asked if I'd go with him down to the ocean.

The windows were open, a light breeze. I read and stretched out on his sofa. "I'm too broke," I said. "You go ahead. Go alone."

"Girlfriend, it's not a *hotel*. It's our summer flat."

"For real?" I said.

"You don't think I'm just leaving you here?" He sat next to me.

"I'm too broke," I said.

"Yes, we know. I can't leave you here, though. You'll start cleaning."

"Fuck, shoot me. Christ. Someone's not listening to me, man."

"Nor me, I think, precious. If you want, you quit."

"Here it is. Here comes the burn."

Luc had a place near the village edge high up the cliffs at the coast in Sperlonga. From the bus stop, the only way to get there those days was to walk. But now there's an access road, and any loud idiot can drive there, to that perfect world. We walked up through olive groves filled with cicada buzz, up a dusty lane, to the whitewashed and honeycombed village. Some roofs were tiled; otherwise the whole place seemed carved from a block of chalk, a single, white, elegant structure, as if cliff-dwelling hermits or bees lived there.

I'd thought such places were just for the lucky few. And I was right. It was just olive groves, us, and young fishermen. I was saved! Forget what I've said before. I saw that life could be paradise. We'd make love, and I'd want nothing more but to choke him to death where he slept. I got used to it.

"Get up," I'd say.

"Oh, let's rest."

"Come on, get dressed. Let's do something."

"Do like what?"

"Something where I can stay *dressed* for five minutes."

Most of the time we were happy, though. We sat in

an open taverna in the village square, and everyone knew what we did. Scrubbing every wall, quietly lost in their witchcraft, the old women grinned at us, and the pious smelled the sex on our bodies, almost scowling, and the girl there kept pouring us wine.

I'd ask him, "Do we want to swim or just *eat* all day?"

"Eat all day."

"And later swim?"

I tried everything. Kiwis, pink cheeses, these peppered figs, buttering the warm sticks of bread.

He rested his feet in a bridge on my legs.

"Hey, don't," I said, "baby, you're crowding us."

"Stupid me. Perhaps we could stay here and live here some?"

"Eat all day. Let me guess—and after that, you'll want some head while I'm under the water."

"Si, nell' acqua," he whispered. "In the water."

"You're like one of those ratty-ass stray cats in heat," I said. ". . . Oh, come on. I'm kidding. You'll live." I would say something wounding to stab his heart, and he would pay the man whatever it was.

Then one day Luc wanted to swim down to the caves. Below his house, the empty beach curved to another hill, a rocky place, jutting out, worn by the ocean. A secret world. The cave was far off, and the waves were cold, but he swam out in clear, briny, verdigris ocean, past the sparkling surf, and around the brown cliffs to the mouth of the cave, calling for me. The cave became shallow as I entered, sloshing after him, and in the dark, a hollow plop echoed on water. I heard wading. Then my eyes grew accustomed to the greenish light. Luc was naked and dripping and seemed to be coalescing out of the air, slowly visible, wringing his bathing suit dry. His cock looked small. "My Speedo, it's all full of sand now," he said.

We waded this grottoed cave shaped like a theater, with crude, sculpted seats. The water going deeper as we waded in. Walls of rock mazed under water.

"You know this emperor, *Tiberio*?" He waved his arm.

"Not that much."

"Here was his small *coliseo*."

"Like a coliseum."

"—In fact, there were animals that fought in this water. And, you know, some slaves. The cave was carved making a *theatro*."

He stepped with the shyness some men can have naked, and he took my hand so he could lead me. We were sopping wet, his fingers all claylike and wrinkled. He was trying to keep me exhausted, almost liquefied!

A staleness there. I needed to run out and get air.

I walked a ledged walkway around the cave, sugar-sand glittering from the entrance where the waves missed. Bowls of green light bounced around on the ceiling rock, freezing, then eddying again with another wave. The cave filled with air, as if the place breathed with the water, for millennia, and we were inside of its mind.

A butcher house.

It got me all sleepy to think of it. The Caesar Tiberius and his retinue, the mosaic pools. I tried to imagine the tyrant king, drunk at his table and vomiting. Then eating again. He orders his Christians killed, lets down the robe from his gut for an orgy. Around him, the rocks and walls splattered with gore, the bloodied slaves. Then he calls all his children in. *"Look what your mother's caused now,"* he says, as he lovingly touches each child on the head.

The badness around us, you could taste it. It got me high. "Whew, it really stinks."

Peering down, I could make out where stone rooms or dungeons had been, in these deep pits of bottle-green water.

Luc squatted on a mossed seat of limestone and paddled his feet in the water. "Come sit," he said, echoing. "What do you think was right here?"

"Who the hell cares," I said. "It's weird in here." I could smell sulfury eggs. I got nauseated, tossing rocks into the water, bombing little fish. "Hey, wait," I said. "Wait, let me picture Tiberio. Like that movie, right? Malcom McDowell in *Caligula*. He'd screw everyone— hack up his slaves and then, what, he'd swim?"

Luc toed at the water and stood shuddering. "*Dio!* It's *cold* down there. Ice water."

"Oh, you don't want to swim now?" I said. "It's a picnic here. Our own private love palace. What the hell."

He crooked his legs clumsily through his bathing suit and squished it on. "Pig," he said. "This place smells dirty. I like to leave."

"What for?" I said. "No one can see us. It's our private pool. Now we can do it again in the water. *Get in*," I said.

"*Andiamo.* I don't like to stay here," he said.

"But I want to swim."

"Let's leave," he said.

"Chicken shit. What were you thinking of, bringing us here?" I stepped by him close to the ledge. You could smell things somewhere, like a stagnant pool. Then I whipped around, feeling his hand touch the back of my shoulder. *"Don't fucking crowd me!"* I said, and Luc almost fell into the water, drawing back a step. My head went hot. "Luciano, stop crawling all over me! Make some room."

I bent down to strip and looked back at him. "And you can have back this ridiculous Eurotrash Speedo." I tossed my trunks.

Then he punched me hard right in the kidneys.

"Hey, you don't do that!" I said.

He stood over me, waiting it seemed. "How do you say? *'That's what you motherfucking get.'*"

I walked the ledge pretending my side didn't hurt. It dawned on me bit by bit. A handful of seats like a porno theater. The smaller scale. An idiot could reach out and touch it, where bad happened here. Carved from the floor by my very feet headed this walkway that ended in water. I touched the pool. It was cold down there. Yet what you felt wasn't a coldness, not *colder*, but an instinct for what had been left. A thought you had. Essence.

The dampened air—I couldn't believe I'd been hit! Everything seemed to infect me. That year I'd just slept out illegally. I trespassed and hid out on all these historic grounds, behind shrubbery, in rat holes you would not want to imagine. I slept everywhere, and I'd sensed something like this before. Back home, in the swamps where I hid when I'd done some wrong. At old Gettysburg. I had felt this feeling at Alcatraz. Salisbury Tor. At Delphi. Megiddo. The lightning field. Vero Beach. This is where people were dead.

"Oh, I'm not so nice, now?" I said. "What's the rush?"

Luc held his arms from the water, looking back at me, and waded out into the day.

This was long ago.

Now I wouldn't know how to find him, or where to go. But I ran through these thoughts as I watched him swim, an odd sort of bad-movie fantasy—of me reaching down under the water as I swam to him, and bashing his brains in with one of those rocks.

It got shallow. He left the surf. So I reached down and that's what I did. I plowed into him.

He went down and he wouldn't get up. He just held his head.

The ocean was purring, and it called me back into its salty womb, mothering us. I waded back into the water.

Irritable, restless, my molars hurt. But lying in his bedroom, I had started to almost feel like a person again. Instead, I hitched back to the fields, to that lightning field. A hallowed ground, whoever knew?

Later I found out that the Allies and the Wehrmacht had fought a bad battle there, losing hundreds of lives on either side. Or perhaps, earlier there, priests had burned pagans and witches? How does a plot of the ground rebel? All I know is I lost my good boots in the lightning, in an utter dark. When things like this happened I cursed God. Then immediately, I would see the far lights of a semi. This happened *again* and *again* out alone like that, and suddenly, here comes some saving light.

I was all screwed up.

Somehow, inside me, my heart lit up. Then it stopped. It wasn't the way he talked. It wasn't about this one guy. He could have been anyone, any of them. But he was the same as you and I.

Floridita

My dad talked to us from the war, the one on the news at night, on an old reel-to-reel Mama kept in the kitchen. She gathered us up, her babies, her two pretty pies, to listen at the tape, airplanes and artillery and the sound of chain on metal muffling my dad's words. "Listen at your daddy," she had asked us, cradling Jane.

"Hi Daddy, hi Daddy." My sister talked back to the tape.

I listened. This is when I was just a little bit of a nothing, a little fifty-pound thing, and it was the wiggliest mystery just being alive. My brother, Jim, was off hiding at summer camp. It was darkening up in our kitchen, and I put my chin, my arms around my head on the Formica tabletop and listened in a dark place to my dad. There were the swords in the jungle; there were the great planes of war. He spoke like from a movie as that tape player rattled his talk. A white bulb hung from mosquito netting above him in a tent at night in the jungle. His humongous boots, his horn-rimmed glasses.

"Listen at your daddy. Hear him, baby?" my mother said.

"Hey diddle-diddle, the Jane and the fiddle. . . . That's a Huey long range setting in."

"I hear," I said. That's him.

The reel-to-reel spun, and there were helicopters coming in low, slow as hornets, their bellies swelled with soldiers, and the soldier dead. I brushed my toes on the chalky tile, feeling the life of me, the action going crackly on the tape. My dad's voice. All hollow, and large in a closed-up way. Closed-up like it was spoken through those small speakers on the car windows at the drive-in. The louder you would turn it, the worse it came out. Me and Mama and Jane were all on top of it, listening to him.

"*. . . Sometimes it's ice cream. Today, I guess, it's some kinds of meat. They fly stuff in like it's Christmas. Oh, yeah, did I tell you we'll transfer up North to Luc Dao? The Highlands are quiet, but it's still the same party, I hear.*"

My mother told us to hang still a second, and she snapped off the reel-to-reel. She went to their bedroom, then came running back with her cigarette case and poured us all some Coke in these shiny tin glasses we had, each one with its curved-out lip a different bitter, steely color.

"*Jim, you and Nimy pay attention to your mama. Your mama's the one who's boss for now. You listening?*" Daddy says.

My mother's lips go pursed up small; she bites them, and then her eyes get squinchy and Mama hides her hurtful face from me. I do my mouth the same way, at Jane, who purses up her littler mouth while watching me. Her legs bounce on her chair under the table, and Dad asks do we hear him good, back here.

"*You rascals. You watching your lovely mother? Are you all children behaving yourself? I miss you critters. . . . Whew, Lordy. Oh, whoa,*" Dad says, and we can hear him hush and breathe. "*Wait puppies. . . I'm gonna stop here for a second.*" Then Dad doesn't say much else, and there's just his breath breathing out on the sound awhile.

Jane answered she was three, holding her few dumb, little-kid's fingers at the black machine. My mother's beehived red hair rocked like all one piece, and she laughs, her hands lighting down on our shoulders now mothered together in this laugh. I drew back inside me. I knew some things. I was always the sassy one; I was the mister-big-britches. No one was pulling the wool over me.

"Who came in Mama's room when she was dressing?" she would say. "Who's her little pretty-pie?"

You could hear Dad breathing on the tape, and waiting, like he was trying it out in his head before he would say something into the tape. They never think we hear their breathing.

"Oh, kids, things aren't so bad, they're not so terribly, tolerably bad. . . . It's hot. Sometimes out here the nights are long. Mosquiters eat your ankles."

"Dad," I breathed on the table, the air warm from my mouth, turning wet. "Come home already, Dad." It sounded like he was maybe on the phone right then and there, at the A&P. "Come home and take us out for a car ride, you and Jane and me and Mom."

My dad talked to us after being gone for months. For what seemed ever. Until it seemed that that's where he was supposed to be. The tough part wasn't us missing him after he had gone, but the big waiting, the day onto day—when he said he'd soon be coming back. Gone was easy. The coming back is what was always hard.

What else did I hear that I remember?

There were these rackety, toolbox things—like men with shovels, and giggly coughing. I hear some men walking by, asking something. But I don't know just what it is they say, in the background, getting closer, then getting farther and farther away. I hear some Coke cans snap and fizz. Them laughing. Hard toy-tiny men, and there's a space around these things, darkish, where Dad talks, or had talked, I guess, his sound lifting off from that penny-brown tape.

—Dad says it will only be a little bit more. That President Johnson's going to get him out. *"Oh . . . soon, soon, before the spring gets here. It's wet in spring. The rainy time. Hey, when it rains it pours."*

We'd turn the television up when Johnson spoke. Every night at supper we watched the news about the war. You could even see the fighting, like a movie, tanks, and helicopter things, and shooting. I wondered if I'd see my dad during parts about the choppers—bullets trickling down like opened fists full of chalky gravel. We pretended we were planes. Always after cartoons there'd be the news about the war: helicopters lowering to let out soldiers over a grassy field, the high grass fanning back beneath the helicopter's props. Then parts about the hippies painted and crazy-wild up north, the TV's war. I'd tell my friends that Dad was in the jungle flying missions. I had his LT cap, and my mother let me wear it so I could prove it to them at school.

I'd show them, holding my hand like a chopper. "This is how he says he shoots them. Look it, this is where the bullets go."

Dad says the biggest thing, the worst of it is nothing much for them to do. The in-between times are boring. But he says that this will change when he gets transferred north to Luc Dao. My dad's voice, then, goes sour on the tape. It's his poutful, huffing voice. He sniffs, and I want to turn the recorder off. I want my mother to talk to Dad and make him happy as a puppy. Mom could fix wherever it hurt. My dad could lift me up and dust me off, but he could never bring himself to kiss the spot on me that hurt. That's who he was. Him. My dad.

We sat at the shaky kitchen table, shaky like all our

trailer furniture—sat and listened to him talking on the snaking loop of tape, a sound like when he'd come home tired, ragged, full of fight from working, the big airfields in Pensacola, Okinawa, Corpus Christi. I remember the white of his T-shirt under his crunching leather jacket. Me and Jim and Jane would ride in his lap and try to listen when he read the paper, when he did the funny comics and read us funny paper news. "Up here, now, midgets," he would say. "Up here on Dad's old bony lap." I could tell the voice Dad made when he was feeling moody. When he slammed around and cursed the Lord, tossing things, hurling metal, machinery things and vacuum tubes, junk, small tools in and around our carport and the ragged yard beyond. Pliers, I remember catching the light, whirligigged out of the car onto our driveway like some shotgunned dropping bird—Dad clomping around from room to room in search of dirty pilot laundry, the back porch, the bedrooms, and the halls. I remember our trailer almost rocking, like it would near about burst apart and scatter us stunned out on the yard grass, the whispers when I listened to them, to Mama and Dad at night.

Dad whispering, Mama kind of whining. Then both of my parents laughing over something we barely heard.

She would come in and check on us when their noises got done at night.

And I'd be faking like I was gone-to-sleep. Some nights, those nights when I was afraid of mostly missing something, I would carry in my pillow and say I'd had a nightmare while I'd listened to them laugh. I'd call her. Those times, my mother would put me in the middle. My dad's big knees like the bumpers on an old car, but hotter, rougher. I'd get the jitteries being brushed by all his hair. But still, it was Dad's hair, Dad and Mama's, and their warm was different than any other warm, a smothering, mouth-sweet warm with their grown-up breath on my smaller breathing. I would have to turn away from him to my mother to get good air.

Other nights my mama would cry, and Dad would get up and stomp outside and slam the doors shut silly, tottering our toys, and pictures dropping. He'd get in our Falcon and drive on off and not be home till he got back. And on worse nights there was fighting. And screaming. In the Bible there is a place that Mama read us where she'd marked. Her thumbnail scratched the pages as she whispered her words and wept. "The marriage is honorable, and the bed undefiled, but whoremongers and adulterers, God will judge," my mother read, "in a lake of fire. Jesus . . . it says that He'll forgive *him* even this. Adulterer like his Daddy." You could hear her drag her nail and watch it dent across the page. The sound! Like something in your dresser, crawly-sized.

More than once, Jim and I went with Dad when he'd go out riding in our car. We'd park outside some bar and Dad would go in for a minute. *"I'll be back in just a minute. Just a second, boys,"* he'd say.

But, me, I wouldn't say anything. Jim would sleep, and I'd sit there quietly peeking for my dad and acting like I was coloring till he got back from where he'd been.

We listened to him talking. How was school, and all that business? How did Jim and I do in the Peanut League?

"—I hate it, Dad. I quit it, dummy! Don't you even know?"

"You children, I don't have much tape left here—so we'd better be getting finished. But hey, now, hold on here a second. Who is Daddy forgetting, hm? Hey, diddle-diddle, the Jane and the fiddle. . . ."

Jane leaned over our table and touched her tongue to the reel-to-reel.

"Mustn't, baby sister. Sit and listen," my mother said. She relit herself a snubbed-out Kool. It was night almost all the way outside, a slap of blue with clouds over the woods behind our ratty park. Our milky-green, automatic streetlights flickering on with their secret minds. I tell Dad to come home right this minute, and my mother smiles at the reel-to-reel. She says I shouldn't be in such a hurry to see our dad. Her eyes go squinty where she's been smoking.

"Shush," I say to her. "It's Daddy. We're not supposed to talk." I watch the tape die out—unrolled—to just roll back in its circle on that dusty reel-to-reel.

We're tired. It makes me sleepy to hear him.

"*. . . All right, well, when am I headed home? Oh soon, mid-January or something. Three months. Sure, soon enough,*" he said.

"No, not then! Not January, dummy."

My mother goes, "There's something, hon', about your daddy. . . . Something we better get clear a bit. Oh, Otis," she goes to the tape. "Aw, honey. What the hell," she said.

My mother squeezed Jane tighter to her—one of

her hands with her short lit cigarette doing spark trails at its end. Jane got to hear the Brer Fox in the briar patch story, and to me he says, *Be a good boy-midget and listen to them at school.* Nothing about the wiggly, not-right feeling in his voice. The feeling in the air around the table as we listen to the tape. And then, with roll to spare, he says he has to talk to Mama now. *There's something that your mother and me must sit down and discuss.*

I'm with Jane and Mama in the kitchen wanting to raise hell with them, and this is how it goes. Believe it? This is how it goes with us, as if I don't already know.

Before my mother goes back to listen to him, to have our Dad alone, he says hello to her like this, like he never does: *"How are you, Floridita? What are you up to, now?"* he says. This is how he talks to her, like it isn't her or him.

Mama said be still and saddled Janey on my lap. She takes the dusty reel-to-reel and goes off small into her room.

She doesn't turn her room light on.

Grocery day was Fridays after school. Those Fridays, that's when we'd meet Lloyd. Lloyd worked the package store where Mama bought her liquor and Cokes for drinking. I never saw my mother drink. My father, I saw. I saw him. Not my mother—or only in the evening, just a little. I sat beside her in our car. She bought me off, her little monster. Quiet. Ice-cream-coned or Crackerjacked and smugly coloring planes.

My mother checking her makeup in the rearview, doing her lipstick face just so. And then, like so.

She'd smack my leg and say, "Let's say hello to Lloyd. Hey, let's go and visit him a second. You like Lloyd, now, don't you baby?"

What was he like, our stepdad, Lloyd?

He was round and red and smelled like limes, an icy smell, like the barber's. He was like a barber, but warmer, chocked with coin and toothpick tricks and ways to do a napkin. It wasn't *him*. It was how *she* was. He would hand her that crunched paper sack of things, that grin, like he could eat a rhino with it. Horn, hair, hoof, and all. And she would put these bottles down between us on the seat—pushing me to over *there*. Away to the door, and off of her.

Her white arm laid out bridged across the padded

steering wheel, her armpit bared—the peppered patch of chicken skin that's hidden under there. You could touch, almost, her dampness. Mama's smell. Her cheeks all pinched up, blushing. I waited while they jibber-jabbered and did their boring talking. Me unthreading tufts of nylon from her nubbed-up toy-green blouse. Me logy-headed and jittery and waiting in the sun. Wanting to put my two-cents in, all fitful, turning cranky, and me just spraddled sideways on our car seat, listening there.

I didn't have to listen long to people. I'm not dumb.

There was once this rainy night when my mother took us in our car, no makeup, raincoat, or umbrella. Just "Go and get inside the car." We drove to some-body's tidy, one-car house, a woman friend of Dad's. We parked in her tiny one-car driveway. Mama hollered, her beehived hairdo hanging out the window of our car. Then she started honking the horn, and Dad drags out with a can of beer. I didn't know halfway what was going on, but when Dad got in she slapped him. I was small and I remembered little. Sure, we drove away. Mom hollered. The dome light lit above me and a car door opened to roaring. *Maybe* Dad pushed her. Or I don't know, maybe it was Mom who jumped out after all. But this I do remember. We all began crying, and Jim reached over the car seat, holding on to her, I thought. Then Mama shouted and grabbed at her door and flew out over the road.

Mom. When I was small, I knew that I was small, and I loved Mama and Dad and I also knew that they were who they were, and I was small when they were very big. When they talked, they talked big, and when they moved, they moved even bigger.

Sometimes things were broken. No, not broken. What things we had were shattered.

—Lloyd was talking and she was laughing the way she did with him, and about what, who can tell, him leaning on her door, his waxy red, clean-shaven face. His key ring jangling on a pair of dice. A shirt with that plastic thing in the pocket for his pens. And hair—short, brindly, broom-straw hair like a greased shoe brush. They jibber-jabbered laughing. I listened. I lay my head on the metal door, looking out, and up. And above me was a sky so deep I could fall in such a sky with big, fat, rolling-over clouds you could lose yourself in for years. And who was her little pretty-pie now?

Goddamn it. Who's the mister-big-britches? Oh yeah, smart-Alex? Who's the sassy one?

I sat there looking up and out. Above me, there was a great plane of war, or just some dumb, old, airline plane.

Dad talked to us way back before the Tet Offensive came—and back before everything else that was awful, or was even worse, to come. He said that he was sorry he was gone.

I believe he was.

"I'm sorry, kids. I'll make everything better if you want me to," he said. *"Your dumb dad does the best he can."*

He says that hurtful father stuff, that he had always done the best he could, and this was in his *tired* voice. Not the poutful, but the wanting one. Our mother starts to answer him. She holds both hands across her mouth—and I swear it—it looks like she is about to fall, and that scares me more than any of this. But then she makes her faking smile and brings herself around. She lights another cigarette. She's back, we're safe, our mom.

"Otis," she says.

165

"Aw, Daddy," we say to the tape.

"We've got the big warm jets coming in, our backup. Listen, can you hear them land?"

"Hi Daddy. Hi Daddy." Jane goes like this, again, but she, my sister, was way too little. She never heard the dishes shattering, bad nights, on our walls.

—Our neighbors coming in to talk to them, the lightning flash of cop-car lights that popped across our yard. Outside, that radio squawk in blue-light darkness. The man that took our dad into the blue-light of that car.

When the baby-sitter came and made the popcorn bag for me and Jim and snugged us down to watch TV—my sister Jane was just a baby. She was in the crib alone in Dad and Mama's room. This was in the house in Corpus Christi. Jim and Jane and the sitter, too, had been asleep for hours when I got on my Spiderman pj top and sneaked into the kitchen.

When I padded in and shut the door and pawed down in our garbage.

When I got out the glue, the one that had the cow on it, and put the cup together. When I left it on our table, the best I could.

"Be good, and mind your mama. I give you all big

Eskimo kisses on the nose till I come home. You midgets, rug rats! Pups," he said.

We listened to my dad tell us to mind our pretty mother, telling us about the rains, the jets, and strange things he had seen off in the buggy jungle there. But he had never really told us what was *happening* in the war. Some things—those things that had to do with us—he never said out loud. The girlfriends, drugs, and other stuff.

This is how our father was.

My dad spoke to us from the war somewhere away from us is all. His echoey breath filling all of those U.S.O. tapes, or he hushed to a hum of static. Dad talked to us like that, like you could almost tell what he wanted to say, by just what he was leaving out.

Not his words, the little things, but the big quiet. The in-between. It was in this kind of blank-spaced quiet that my mother came back with the reel-to-reel. A Kleenex tucked half out of her blouse, that wet in her eyes and their rawness. Her own mom-quietness larger than anything she would now say. We wouldn't move or could barely much speak.

I thought, *Hey, Mom!* I wanted to shout it. *Hey,*

Mama, cut it out, okay? Jane wiggled back in her chair a bit and put nearly all of her fist into her mouth. She gnawed herself, each tooth like the tips of small corn. Then Mama clicked on our kitchen light. I thought— I wanted to con her—*Hey, Mama, wait a minute,* I'd say. Let's send Dad a brand-new tape and tell him we're all fine. Let's tell him we'll take our Falcon out for a ride when he gets back. And tell him how Jane and I will sit real quiet until we're all the way home again—tell him how we could maybe even stop for drinks. Nothing like coming on home at night, asleep, with Mom and Dad driving. So still, so rushy and quiet.

I thought it, but I didn't say.

We would watch to see him on the TV news at night.

My mother laid down the reel-to-reel and plugged it behind our table. "Let's tell him. Let's say good-bye to Daddy, now," and this is all she said.

Who's Your Daddy Now?

Out here, these rich people's places keep everything stony and old, the way it maybe was, oh, a billion years ago, but that just makes me think of ghosts, of these houses all drafty and atticked with the crap left from their dead. They ride in my backseat while I'm driving, hating my mind and despising life.

I drive around. This is what things have sunk down to, rotation: I skip around watching for stations where I've yet to bother for my dollar of gas.

I park. There's the three-story house with old cupolas, a fake widow's walk. I'm expected, but I can't see which door to use. I look in my sideview mirror, but nobody's there, just a glittery sludge in the bowl of the glass, my palm, a ghost-me in my mirror. Clean fatigue jacket, fucked-up hair. My comb has dropped back to the dark with my pennies and my hope down the crack of the dash, down there, where your razors and things fall between the walls to unreachable voids in the world. *You fraud! You can't even get combed for a job*, each wall, each room, and every window of this house it seems is saying. Hear it? The wind at the back of the house with the whispery hall.

On water. The yard ends in beach sand and sea grass. A setter barks chasing a sword-tailed pheasant. A wine bottle left in a birdbath. Hid in grass, one high-heeled shoe. All pillared, these East Hampton houses tomb-white from the dunes. A bum thumbs on the roadway, ragged in khaki. Kiting gulls.

Not too many jobs are left here on the coast, and as usual, I'm down to roofing or yard work. Mostly Vet stuff. Gigs like this.

My side of the walk-around porch with the door by the drive I figure is best. I'm sweating. I'd put the two extra holes in my belt with a nail.

This lady, she doesn't even open the door. She's

horsey, silver-haired, maybe around sixty, underfed. Yet the first thing I think is would she want to give me some head? Would I want her?

Yeah, sure. I've never been fit much for work.

"Hey, you're backward—why are you knocking here?" she says.

I tell her I tried in the front.

She's trashed. Her fingertips frog on her side of the glass.

"I phoned," I say.

"Well, this is not a usable entrance. Come on in, but mind the pots."

I come on into the porch. "What pretty hibiscus," I fake like I'm nice.

"They're healthy, huh? I like to plant if I don't have to weed. We'll drag all these babies inside on cold nights, but you can't set them close to the fire. . . ."

I've got her! To hex her I pinch at her poppies, hike and scratch my drooping socks—like magic, my life is carried away in that gesture. I'm Mr. Calm. "Could repot a tad. Feel this old dry rot," I say.

Oh God. Does she picture me weeding and watering things I was already starting to dread?

"Yes, well... So you sound like you *might* be a gardner. Were you in the service?"

"Once," I say.

"No problems to mention, or otherwise."

"I'm thinking. None like *that*," I say.

I fill out some paper with names of old relatives, churchy types. Swear that I work like a dog.

"No horseshit. You are either a crook or you're not. Whichever. A room is offered over the car barn, since summers you're alone to see everything's kept."

"Your pipes and such."

"There are sodas for you in the larder. I trust you don't smoke while you're, you know, in bed."

"I've never checked."

"What?" she says.

"No, I quit smoking," I say, then the panic hits. I figure this lady sees clear to the nub. I hide it. You can't have them knowing how hollow you are when they're peering inside at the fear. She nods for me then to look outside to the car barn. Something's there, and strangely a pheasant falls out of the air, its head electrical and twitching, feathered brilliant metal green.

Ms. Whitney, she tells me our hands are in God's.

I came by her job through my drunk uncle, Skippy,

who knew her from newcomer nights at A.A. It's one of their perks you can get if you're sharp, some work, and the coffee they crank by the tub. I'd heard it all, everyone waiting to be saved.

We shake, and she signals me out through her door.

Before leaving, I glance up from toeing the lawn. Upstairs, with her hand tapping *hi* from a window—peeking out—is this skitty girl. An arty type, hair in a big nest of curls. Then she turns into glare and just disappears. This rotten job. Around me the faces and spirits are trying to shapen themselves from the air. I could use a beer.

I wonder, what if I had a decent life? And I drive it in back of the yard.

Here's something to try when applying for work. It's a trick that I do to relax. It's simple: just picture you have already worked there before. Put a memory-you on the porch. You're settled—you've lived here forever pretend. A local—imagine you know all the words! Then act like the *boss* is the stranger to town who you judge with the neighborly dead.

That khakied bum walks by on our road. I notice, since everything else is on wheels—Mercedes, and that type of millionaire ride. Not thumbing, he slouches beyond his "unsightliness" off into utterly nothing at all. Near gone, not a rag on the sandy landscape. By our roadside, island pines. I'm fine, and Ms. Whitney's out bombed at her brunches, her clubs, with the daughter inside at the TV all day with a boyfriend, being stoned.

I garden and keep a sharp eye on the place while the Whitneys do their play. But now I'm fishing dead rats from the rain gutter drain where they all crawled up to eat each other. A smell, well yes, like death, and a kind of cheese. It's terrible, all that can get at your life. The violence. The razors piled back of your medicine cabinet are rusted in one hideous blade.

I've been to where no one was sure if his luck was still there or was holding us long on this earth. You couldn't have. Killers all hid in the trees in the tropical heat. But now I'm fine. Still, I'm always scared something's going to *get me* in one of these old Long Island houses, behind the trees, or on the other side of night—or just these windows—in the hiding dark.

Whatever it is, you can never see *them*, but they can sure see in. Anyways, at least at night.

At night, *this night*, I watch the daughter at her window from the lawn, that flag of lamplight through her window, shadowed panes in a shadow cross. I'm with my cigarettes and bottle. For a cover I'm salting slugs. I toke up a cigarette to spark, then I write out her name with its reddish trail.

Athena.

All earringed, dolled up and hot in her makeup and her rich kid, Zulu clothes.

One morning she watches me through her window, dim and penciled passed the screens. I spook her.

"—Miss Whitney."

"Christ, Otis!" she says. She's chatty now, leaning at her window while I clean the filthy screen. She flirts and sags onto her mattress, watching me. This queen. This kid curling dim in a nap.

"You're up? But it's not even lunch yet," I say.

"I'm just now getting to sleep."

"You puppies."

"... Loser dude," she says.

She can talk while I'm popping her screens. "No way, guy, like where did you get that tattoo?"

"Got me. Aw, I'm lying. It took me years till I drew one I liked. You want it?" I tell her I'll ink her a good one, a heart with her name like the skull on my heel.

"Right here?" and the girl lifts her shirt from her

belly. It's lovely, a fine honeyed delta of fuzz. "Wish on," she says to me. "Not in your scuzzy old dreams."

I'll watch her. It's awesome just watching her think. Her shadowed self shows through her curtains, and once, I even saw her sex, her legs, and the seaweedy ringlets of hair on her freckled back.

Now night, I drink in the letchering darkness, dear Lord God. I swig. In a moment I'm pealing my zipper and squeezing her telescoped into my mind, so close, till her naked and make-believe body is shuttled in pictures between me and her, her daughter-ish body and her laughter, through her window, on the phone.

I work.

I keep hearing "Otis," but no one whenever I turn is visibly there.

Before I've half unplugged the rain gutter drains that bum has returned down our road. Pure vagrant. Just this side of the causeway, a ghost from the grave in his khaki clothes. I load the muck into my bucket leaking water-rust and leaves, go dump it, pretend I don't notice his bumming and smoke up a roach in the rotting wind.

The water's high, waves rolling bottle glass polished to beads, and the surf crushing spray into dust.

What country, here. Everything seems to be breathing, things trying to hypnotize me into calm. They're tricky: the surf washes shallow from blue into Coke-bottle green.

While raking, I notice that bum's on the way back to shore again, but this time he's waving hi.

His face! That sunlight around his head, his eyes— they glitter and shard into light as if he were a crazy man or a wild hound about to bite us.

He waves his hi, and says my name, *I think*, and suddenly I know who it is. Me, I'm on my knees with a hand in the bucket. He slouches up.

Coots! His face is now lost in its shadow, just like God's.

"Hey. Say there, bud. Say buddy." His voice buzzes nearly familiar to me as my dad speaking back from a dream.

As usual, I'm not decided just yet if he's real. He's skittery. I'm sort of scared I might die.

"No, Jesus . . . Coots," I tell him.

He giggles and pinches my arm.

"Shit, Coots. It's true," I say.

177

"Believe it? Imagine us finding us here."

Not anything, *no one* escapes where they've been. I tell him, "Coots, what in hell are you doing? You're not here." I throw down the bucket and grab up my rake. "It's you . . . it was you who was calling my name all night."

"I reckoned I'd wait till you'd hear. Been hunting you. Talked a bit some with your mother . . . says you never call."

I haven't glimpsed him in years. "You're breathing?"

Whenever he drops from my life, I keep guessing that Coots maybe went off and died, then he's back again. Down in Washington once, I looked over to see if his name had showed up on the Wall. I stood there embarrassed in front of the dead, with the terrible ants on the stone in the glare. Me, I walked some point with him back in the service.

We weren't lucky. We all lost.

"Coots, Jesus. How do you track where I'm at? Look, Curtis. Coots," I tell him. "Now, don't you go losing my job."

"I wouldn't."

"You know you can't hang on this road."

"I wouldn't. I wouldn't go doing you wrong."

Coots grabs up some leaves and shakes them off into the bucket.

"So you would've stayed dicking around out there till I maybe waved you hi?"

"I might have."

"You look like something that died."

"Near had." His teeth have that sad-looking green, all gapped, like the inky-teeth smile of a clown. "Say, lover boy, you ain't much fitter," he says.

Like most, I once lived alone in the back of my car, though Coots came and stayed, till he brought in the puppy, this soot-bellied boxer he named for his mother. I told him no dogs in the car. It froze. Then we pretty much parted ways.

I see him next morning near Honeycut's store, Coots thumbing, comes wavering up from the heat—he shimmers. A wine bottle flat in his pocket, a filterless Chesterfield back of his ear. One evening he's hitchhiking out by the seawall, I'm driving, the headlighted black road macadam is snowed with sand. I honk it and tell him to hop in my Dodge. "No kidding, they'll throw you in jail if you're not in a Volvo."

"A Acura."

"—If you're white or not. They could care less."

"But I'm a veteran."

"That's *worse* out here," I say. I tell him I know he camps nights in the cornfield, and that I can be bribed to let him help me—the mowing and painting—if Ms. Whitney okays.

"Can't allow it."

"Coots, hop your ass in and come on."

"Down in Merrick," Coots rattles, "are stables to muck, out on Chesapeake, shucking clams. Heck, anything. I ain't for selling my blood, those fuckers. They run me off I-ninety-five."

Getting seated, Coots reaches as if he would pat me and pinches the crap nearly out of my arm. Coots winks. He slaps up some dust from his pockets. "You buying? A man shouldn't go without change when they's cans on the highway, five whole cents."

"You've give me a blood blister, darn it," I say.

Already he's snagging my change from the dash.

I sneak him outside in the pink of the morning and hope that Athena won't see through the side-window screens that I peek in at night.

It's like that. Things seem to just drop in my lap.

I hide Coots a few nights in the car barn attic, until he hits the road.

━

Once, while bleaching their blinds, I caught some boyfriend and her on the floor. Athena, her hair in a mermaiding fan on the rug and a scrawny, rich boy-friend on her. She sees me, her butt off the floor with their heaving like they're both nearly heart-attacked, ready to come. The next thing I catch is their sandwich bag, and the butaney smell of burnt cotton and coke with that Styrofoam smell of its own. As always, the freebase could feel I was watching, so I just glanced back at the classy spread. The pillows, the partylike scatter of cigarettes, mirror, the Heinekens, razors, the blow.

It's crazy, now *I'm the one* feeling all foolish, and head to the barn like I'm walking on snails. Athena, her skirt at her waist while they laugh, and with him on her.

"Sorry," I tell her, "I got all confused. I still kind of go sort of spacey when I see something strange."

—Like fate. Which in actual truth, I saw: *butaned, an Athena as an angel in flames on our harbor road. She runs, her hair shedding droplets of flame.*

"Okay, okay," she says. "But you watched. Well,

what the hell, Linc had to bolt anyhow. You busy? So you like to toot up some coke?"

"Not really. But wait, let me get my cigs," and et cetera. The curtains breeze open to watch. You can feel it, no one at home but the nervous in here, and our whisperings, me and her. I'm dying. With women it's like this at first, before it: they *won't* let you know if you're winning it seems, and you *can't* let them know when you're scared.

It's terrible, all that can get at your life.

I shudder from dreaming I'm getting away—and I wake. I wake and I'm still just me.

Come Saturday, Coots and I sit in a coma, a six-pack of Colt .45 on the porch. We've worked near from dawn until straight up through lunchtime at crabbing out Augustine grass on our knees. We're buzzed, with the Whitneys away until Monday to sail with some golfer up Provincetown way.

They've never seen Coots sneaking back in the attic. They never hear anything more than the owls. My pal, we wipe out the weeding by evening that we had this weekend to do for my chores.

He's off a bit. I don't deny that he's odd. To start with, Coots never is where you'd expect him and is never not smoking or swigging a beer. By Sunday we've bagged up the crabgrass and sit with our cigarettes, breeze in our hair. Coots pops me a tall one and sags to his rocker. I lob off our empties to fall on the grass by the garbage bags. Across the corn brake and the beach grade sounds of laughter in the night, the silent car barn with its giant yawn.

Collapsing, Coots lies on the porch. "God help me if I'm nearly worn to the cob."

"I'm useless." I slide to my back on the glider. I squash out some beer to my mouth from the can.

My buddy sits forward, gone dark in his shadow. He expertly hoots out a call to our owls. "It's funny, huh, us ending up nothing much."

"I planned it," I say. "I can't figure out why the effort."

"Sooner shoot myself as slave like we did in the Highlands. We're worthless. But ain't it like us after all?"

"I guess so. My luck seems to drop from the sky."

"Like birds shitting. God must look out for the shiftless."

Like Indians, a whippoorwill answers his call. He's muttering. "Sometimes I think I feel Jesus. He's just hanging there, eyeing things."

His face! His face in the dark flattens silhouette-like as he wills fading out of our light.

"Hey knock it off. Coots, don't you start being spooky. Don't go weird."

Coots settles. "Say, isn't this dark like Tra Nang?"

It's starless out. I tell Coots it is.

"It looks like everything dark is just trees."

I could hear them. I could hear the young killers all waiting for me just to shoot them, hid deep in the leaves. I suck out the suds, then toss my can in the yard, and I tell Coots it does.

Coots asks for a bottle of Ms. Whitney's good vodka. "I saw it, there, back up the freezer," he says.

"You go on ahead. And get us her cash while you're at it. Hell, torch the place, and think of how else you can help us."

I give up.

As I'm talking, Coots fingers this wet, matted mouse from his pocket flap and drops it in my lap.

"Oh, Jesus, Coots! Come on," I say.

"Going to getcha . . . *Aw, come on. Aw, come on,*" he says. "Come here, little feller." He palms it up.

I'm tired and we're making a mess. I can't handle it. "To hell with the Whitneys," I tell him. "Hey, buddy, let's have us this teeny last beer." I'm finished, but Coots, he never stops. Playing his mouse like a puppet he dances it right up beside my mouth.

"Aw, come on, aw, come on," like that, he goes. "Kiss it!"

It dawns on me. Everyone here is half nuts except, maybe me.

Like always, I fall, passing out down a tunnel, my mind reeling backward not caring at all. While sleeping, I dream I'm the ghosts in the attic, a haunt in the ceiling, the howl in our corn. Weird things, but I *mostly* dream I'm with Athena. We're all guilty, same old stuff.

Come daybreak, I'm barely winked good into sleep, then I wake, my neck covered up in a curtain and damp girly laundry on me on the porch. Great rubbery bulbs beat the headachey blood in my brain through these crumbling, tiny veins. I've blown it, though I don't know just yet what I've blown. I barely don't recollect knowing this ceiling, which might, for a moment, be home with my mom.

Ms. Whitney. Her voice cuts the peace from the edge of my sleep like a knife scraping chrome from a car. She clomps her car door definitely shut and surveys her yard with our beer can garbage. I blink up. To horror. A car wreck of bented-up beers by the leafy bags. She asks do I mind interrupting my nap, would I awfully mind much if she were to ask me what all in the good holy fuck have I done?

Enough.

I tell her I just fell asleep, that I must of been napping: I'm mowing the lawn. She screams at me. Roars through the porch with her screaming. "You. Out of here, I can't be running a flophouse! What—good Lord in heaven—what's that smell?"

I flinch a tad. "Maybe the yard got me sick."

I'm fired.

She leaves me toweled up with a sheet in the sobering breeze.

Just off from me, just out of reach in my vision is swimming this clear gnatty hydra of dots. I give a swipe. Cruddy things fly by my eyes.

Inside through the screen, near the head of the table, I see Coots. He's hatless, his hair standing patchy and half cut. Sunglasses. The tablecloth trashy with beers. Ms. Whitney stands next to her daughter, her mouth wording whispery things as in prayer.

I puke from the porch on some pained-looking violets.

"This party's through."

"Ms. Whitney, it's nothing," I say. I come on in.

"It's better if you don't even bother," Ms. Whitney says. "Let's just make believe you're not here."

"Hey, hidy." Coots offers the women what must be some coffee—in their saucepan. He crooks a scarred arm to shake hands. "So, anyhow, I'm friends of Otis," he says.

"Ms. Whitney. . . ," I say.

Ms. Whitney goes clomping right on up the stairs.

I call, but she never looks back where Coots sits with her stack of fashion magazines.

Him grinning there, dumb as a dog with a shirt on. Then it's done.

I drop him—I shrug him off small as a raindrop. It's like when you're leaving, you send off, or bury somebody. You look up to smile and they're not really there: They're already half forgotten. They still talk, but you're long gone.

"No, he's a dayworker," I yell up the stairs. "Athena, please get her to not call the sheriff." I near like to vomit up into my palm. "Aw Jesus, I just needed help for a day. Look, it's nothing, no big deal. Ms. Whitney? Come look, he just took up and run . . . hey, look it! He's already gone up our road."

Athena leans neutrally, watching him leave. She pops the fridge, reaches inside for a beer. "Malt liquor? Wow. Aren't there some Heinies or anything here?"

October, I've winterized all but the car barn. I've trellised, I've painted their place near nothing, plus for their forgiveness, my rooming and board. Ms. Whitney, I save her the rich people's wages she'd pay if she hired up local folks. The truth is, the rich get as cheap as the poor.

But now I'm fine. It rains, the sea sounds like a drive-in speaker, a clean ocean breeze sweeps the drains. For autumn Ms. Whitney has fixed me the larder, a separate entrance, a bureau, a bed. I do up a barbecue pig for her parties. I wait with her party help ferrying plates. I carry her snoozing upstairs to her bedroom, unshoeing her slippers on rails up the stairs. *"Whoa—you put me down . . . I'm just resting,"* she says, near snoozing, her hair shooting roots under blonde.

At night it is lovely out salting the slugs. A movie

life. Watching the angel Athena inside through her blinds. There's a thing, well, it's weird when I'm watching her think, her dreaming, each jittering move of her body, each shrug, is some scary-like gesture of witness from each of her cells to their being alive, as if maybe her skin thought she'd live here forever all naked in bed with her suede-looking tan. When I'm done with my slugging I smoke on the porch . . . her jewelry, the car keys behind the cushions on the lounger chairs are mine. I nip a bit, tidal wind tossing our corn, a whippoorwill, tide groaning loaded with weeds.

From my bed in the dark in the big stone larder, moonwash lit on the kitchen walls, I watch as a body goes by in the hallway. Through our kitchen, shadows walk. I'm thinking it's *her* maybe walking the dark.

"Say, Otis?" Ms. Whitney walks blue in my room. Her ghost, while my mind tries to make her *her daughter*. I'm awful; I smell her all hopeful in powder, around us a tent of her soggy perfume. She whispers, "Thought maybe you still were awake." Her whisper, like parents somewhere could be hearing and we were their children hid under the stairs. "I'm having a nightcap to get me to sleep. I thought I would ask if you'd care for a drink or not. I thought, well, funny—I can't get to sleep."

"A nightcap."

"Sometimes, I just can't seem to sleep. I pray for it. Just between us and the gatepost. So, who's watching? Want a shot?"

She pours me a rocks glass half with vodka, clinking the bottle a tad on my glass. Too narrow, the larder can't fit us a chair so I scoot to one side and she sits on my bed. It's cool in here, moon slanting blue in the hallway. Through her nightgown, she's all white, all pale, then the darkening mounds of her body. Near her belly, hidden hair. I make her this dried sort of twin of her daughter and mull on the girl fading up through her eyes.

When I reach for my clothes on the floor of the larder I'm handed up only my crumb-covered shirt.

I know this. It's all automatic, the rest. It's simple. She draws up her legs on my mattress. She talks, but I never quite hear what she says.

I stare.

I wait till it's where I should kiss her.

I settle her hand on myself through the sheets.

Out back, I go have me a smoke on the porch. It's quiet, a row of corn tossed in the moonlight. Nothing

190

then. I watch as a cornstalk is shoved with the wind, then next to it, other stalks move in a line, and farther on, dry bony stalks start to wobble.

They bend as if animals ran through the corn. I figure it's Coots playing chase in the cornfield—or him playing army. It maybe is. Coots everywhere, chasing himself in the corn.

All October, I keep hearing someone say "Otis." But no one, whenever I turn, is visibly there.

—I figure she'll write me I'm canned in the morning, a note that her daughter will read as a joke. Her mom, though we both fell asleep with her drool on my arm and I took in her old person's breath. It's true: I am praying we don't wake the daughter. I'm still wanting. I'm that lost. I swear to God, things seem to fall from the sky. I sink near to sleep with my coins on the lounger, go get me a beer, and walk down to the waves. They're spawny, the surf sudsing up in the moonlight, a sound from the waves as if something breathed. Like always, at first I'm afraid of the cold, the deep, all the things in there waiting to eat me, but I've seen worse. I touch the water. I roll up my cuffs and wade out toward the moon in its light on the waves. Amazing, the sounds of the tide on our water.

HEAD

Later, I heard, they found Coots gone cold in some dumped-off car. But I didn't hear this *then*. This coveralled codger walks into the truck stop when I'm down in Tucson, hauling lime. I know the guy. Otherwise everything's quiet, a handful of men in the diner, that desert light, a crockery-red range of low mountains off shuddering miles in the afternoon heat. I'm half through a bacon-cheese plate at the counter, just sitting there hoping I'd get some peace.

He starts in on me. *How you doing, old bud,* and all that.

I'm thinking I won't get to finish.

Dull Texaco patch with his name in red threading, he shifts with his boots as if stuck there in sand. More coffee comes. I ask for more cream in those tiny containers, down Tucson served cool in their small dish of ice.

This fellow, he tells how my friend had been found.

I spoon up the milk curdle flaked in my coffee.

"Worked the both of you trucking," he tells me. "Am I right?"

"Yeah, well," I say, "I'm just here having some coffee," or such as that.

"I just thought," he says.

I don't know *what* it is, really, I say.

But I pick up his lunch tab and drive on to Reno. No big deal. No biggy. Three solid grand a month overnight driving, a sweetie in Phoenix. What was a lunch? Ms. Whitney, she'd said that our hands were in God's. Now they're all gone.

You can see to next Tuesday for all that it matters outside in the stunned Arizona light. I climb it up, high as King Rat in my cab, AC on, and spike off my hot, holstered thermos with a half-a-pint topper of Johnny Black. I take a sip, ulcery, and feel the hooch sour my stomach. I think, better him than me. Then I crank her up. I look in my sideview mirror but nobody's there, not a soul in sight. Just me and God on the highway, for like ever, nothing road. It's like that. Things seem to just drop in my lap. I shift it past nine in that shiny Mack diesel. I flat let her go.

U s

After this, we're breathing in the half-darkness of blue window light, and it still snows. A flurry that taps like salt against the cracked glass in the window to our apartment. Her pillow and the cold sheets crunching together as she stirs.

I'm here, and the room comes back rematerialized. A smell of bread between our legs, my body across her body. I still have my head against her hair, and breathe Chanel, shampoo, and soap from her warm neck. It is not that we're so perfect; her skin feels wet where my breath was. But we're safe. Our heater roars below, and something else. I can hear it, the blood rushing inside of us.

THE AUTHOR

William Tester is a native of Charleston and North Florida, and is the author of the novel *Darling*, published by Alfred A. Knopf. He has degrees from Syracuse and Columbia Universities, and is the recipient of an NEA Fellowship for Fiction, the Hob Broun Prize, the PEN Syndicated Fiction Award, and grants from the Virginia Commission for the Arts and the Constance Saltonstall Foundation. He lives in Richmond and teaches creative writing at Virginia Commonwealth University.

Ken Collins